A Place to Rest

Tom Miller

Legacy Book Press LLC
Camanche, Iowa

ACKNOWLEDGMENTS

This book would not exist without the enthusiasm and steadfast support over many years of my son, David. Born and raised in the last two decades of the twentieth century in Iowa, he was enthralled by my stories of growing up in post-World War II Alabama, a time and place that seemed far away and exotic to him. For almost two decades, he encouraged me to write about that time and place. I wasn't convinced, but while I didn't say "yes," I also didn't say "no." On January 1, 2020, I finally resolved to give it a go. I hope that the result pleases him.

Small presses had published my earlier novels for middle-grade readers, and I enjoyed the close relationship with the publishers. So, I initially sent the manuscript for *A Place to Rest* to three such publishers. Lucky for me, Jodie Toohey of Legacy Book Press LLC liked what she saw and offered me a contract. Jodie guided the book from start to finish with a sure hand. I hope it measures up to her expectations.

Jaime Napurano read and critiqued the early manuscript and provided invaluable advice and encouragement throughout the process. Former Alabama librarians, Alice Stephens and Yvonne Crumpler, offered sage advice and generous support based on their unique perspectives.

My wife, Connie, as always, believed in and supported my work.

Thank you all!

DEDICATION

For Dylan & Ryan

"Life is nothing but an electron
looking for a place to rest."
~Albert Szent-Gyorgi

DRAMATIS PERSONAE

MILDRED MORGAN, Librarian at Wiregrass County (Alabama) High School

JANET BELL, *Montgomery Observer* Reporter and Mildred's best friend

ROGER MORGAN, Mildred's husband, teacher at Wiregrass County High School

JAMES MORGAN, Mildred's and Roger's son and the original Baby Boomer

ERNEST MORGAN, Roger's father and family patriarch

JOE MORGAN, Roger's brother

JOEL STEWART, James' best friend

JOE STEWART, Joel's father and Grover's Fork movie theater manager

PATTY STEWART, Joel's mother

EARL THOMAS, Janet's colleague at the *Observer*

FRANK JACKSON, Football coach at Wiregrass County High School

DICK HADLEY, Janet's college friend

BETTY HOWARD, TV reporter and Janet's friend

COL. RICHARD DEAL, Janet's friend and mentor

MAC, Janet's editor at the *Observer*

MARIE WALKER, James' high school sweetheart

And many others, real and imagined.

CONTENTS

CHAPTER 1
IN THE BEGINNING

"First 1946 Birth in County Announced," *The Wiregrass Herald*, Wednesday, January 2, 1946, p. 6.

Wiregrass County [Alabama] Memorial Hospital announced its first birth of the New Year yesterday. James Chester Morgan, the first child of Roger and Mildred Morgan of Grover's Fork, was born at 12:00 a.m. yesterday, checking in at 7 pounds, 12 ounces, and 22 inches.

The proud father teaches history at Wiregrass County High School in Grover's Fork, and the new mother is the school's librarian. When contacted by the *Herald*, Mr. Morgan said that his son's New Year's Day arrival was quite a surprise. "We didn't expect him for another couple weeks," he noted, "but we're happy he's here. I'm sure that Mildred will tell you that earlier is better than later in these things."

Mrs. Morgan, looking surprisingly alert after a late night, admitted that the early arrival caught her off-guard. "I hadn't even packed for the hospital yet," she explained. "Of course, it's not like

I didn't have months to get ready. Anyway, he's here and he's healthy. That's all that matters."

****

Encyclopedia of the South, Vol. III, p. 236.

Wiregrass: A region of southern Georgia, southeast Alabama, and northwest Florida noted for the widespread presence of Aristida stricta, a coarse native grass known colloquially as wiregrass. The region features hot and humid summers and mild winters. Given its long growing season, agriculture is the principal industry, and cotton is the primary crop, although its traditional dominance is declining in the region. Manufacturing, especially textiles and forestry products, is growing as the area seeks to diversify its economy. Wiregrass County, Alabama, lies near the geographical center of the region.

****

A History of the Alabama Wiregrass, by James Otis, pp. 321-2.

Following the removal of the Creek Indians in the early 1830s, white settlers seeking a new frontier for cotton cultivation flooded into the Wiregrass region. "King Cotton" ruled the region until after World War II when the area began to shed its heavy reliance on the crop. After 1960, agriculture steadily declined in importance as corporate owners, timber companies, and developers absorbed private farms.

****

January 5, 1946

Dear Mildred,

Oh, wow. Congratulations. I'm so happy for you and Roger. I can't wait to see James. Sooner rather than later would be good, but I used the last of my vacation time at Christmas. I'll try to get down some weekend soon though. I know that things are probably crazy there but do try to write a bit. I'm dying to hear all about the birth and James.

Remember back in junior high when we'd debate who'd get married first and have children? I always knew it'd be you. And now, here we are. It seems that I'm no closer now than I was back then. My mother reminds me of that in every letter. We're twenty-four. Is that so old? Of course, my mom already had three kids by the time she was twenty-four. I think that's insane. From her perspective, I'm behind the curve. But she wanted to have a family. Period. I want to have a career. Look at you. You have a career and a family. It's just taking me a little longer. If I'm honest, my social life is not encouraging. You'd think that a society columnist would get out more.

I should go to church. I almost said go to church more, but that's not honest. I haven't been to church since I moved to Montgomery after graduation. You and I seldom went when we were at Birmingham-Southern, but seldom is not never.

You took Dr. Curry for philosophy, right? I know that we didn't take it together. Anyway, I'll never forget the day he discussed Nietzsche. He walked into class that morning, went to the board, and wrote, "God is Dead." The room got very quiet. We were all still good Methodists back then. If I recall correctly, it wasn't so much God that was the problem as it was organized religion. What everyone remembers is that bold statement: "God is Dead." Anyway, I'm not ready to bury my personal God yet, but He's on life support.

Excuse the digression. Anyway, Montgomery is full of men. Maybe even one for me. So, we'll see. Despite mom's prodding, I'm not in a hurry. To find a man that is. If I feel a sense of urgency, it's at work. I knew that I'd have to start at the bottom, but I'm already a better reporter than half the staff. My editor knows it too, but he says I need to be patient. What he means is that nobody likes a pushy woman. I chose this path, and I never expected it'd be easy. I should just probably just shut up and keep grinding. You're my best friend and my only sounding board. Thank you for listening.

You deserve better from your best friend than my whining at a time like this. Maybe I do need a child to remind me that there's something bigger than my dreams.

Kiss James for his "Aunt" Janet, and I hope to see baby and Mom soon.

Love,
Janet

****

January 18, 1946

Dear Roger,

Congratulations from Paradise. Mom's letter with news about James' birth finally caught up to me here in Hawaii. I left China in early January and rotated back to Pearl Harbor. I should be stateside in a couple of weeks and home soon after that. I think it's good that we pulled occupation duty after Okinawa. It gave us a few months to decompress. But I have to tell you, brother, I saw things on Okinawa that I doubt I'll ever forget. I'm glad that you were spared that.

4

When things would get really dicey, I'd remember how Tim Cannon and I couldn't wait to join the navy back in '43. We had no idea what we were getting into. Of course, nobody does. We were afraid that we'd miss the war. I can't even imagine that now. I remember Mom got all teary every time I mentioned enlisting. Dad didn't say much. He was probably happy to see me go. He never expected me to be a farmer. You were his big hope to carry on the Morgan Farms' tradition. But even that wasn't about you. It was about him. Everything is about him.

Tim got lucky, was sent to radio school and spent the war in Hawaii. I thought I was lucky too when I was selected for the Hospital Corpsman School. What I didn't know was that a lucky few graduates of corpsman school are selected to attend the Field Medical Service School to train as Marine medics. Lucky me, right? So, I joined the Navy expecting to serve on a ship with hot food and a warm, dry berth every night and ended up in the mud on the front lines with a Marine company. Life is a crapshoot.

I looked Tim up as soon as I got here, and we got drunk. It seemed like the thing to do. He hasn't decided what he wants to do. He said that the only thing he knows for certain is that he doesn't want to go back to Grover's Fork. Neither of us could wait to leave; now neither of us wants to return. It's not just Dad. And it's not just the farm.

For as long as I can remember, I've wanted something more without knowing exactly what that was. Now, I think I know. I've decided to become a doctor, and I've already applied to the University. If I learned anything out here, it's that I have an aptitude and a passion for medicine. That was a revelation. Before this, the only thing I was passionate about was escaping from Morgan Farms. While that was a goal, it wasn't a destination. The G.I. Bill should cover college. If not, I can always work part-time.

I expect that homecoming will be bittersweet, but Mom will finally be able to relax. This has been hard on her. My second stop will be to see you, Mildred, and my new nephew.

See y'all soon,
Joe

****

"Wiregrass County Unemployment Rate Jumps to 8.5%," *The Wiregrass Herald*, June 5, 1946, p. 1.

The unemployment rate in Wiregrass County climbed 1.5% last month to a post-war high of 8.5%. The local trend still trailed the 8.9% posted nationally. Experts warn that unemployment will continue to trend higher as the military demobilizes and the nation transitions to a peacetime economy.

The Serviceman's Readjustment Act of 1944—a.k.a. the G.I. Bill—offers some cushion for returning veterans in the form of a full year of unemployment compensation. The Bill also provides education assistance, which should take up some of the slack in employment.

Merle Chambers of the local office of the Alabama Department of Labor told the *Herald* that things will likely get worse before they get better. "The economic transition is being complicated by shortages of raw materials in some industries," he noted, "and many industries are hesitant to ramp up production too fast until they can gauge demand."

Jack Nichols of Grover's Fork signed up for unemployment benefits last week after returning home from Panama City, Florida, where he was serving with the Army Air Force. "I'm not sure what I'll do," Nichols said. "I joined the service right out of high school back in '43, so I'm entering the workforce for the first time. I'm thinking about using the G.I. Bill for college if nothing turns up. I never thought there was much chance for me to go to college though, so we'll see."

****

June 12, 1946

Dear Janet,

School's out. Finally. I can't tell you how relieved I am to finally be home all day with James. My mom is great with him, but it was harder than I thought going back to work after he was born. I often found myself daydreaming about him in the middle of the school day. Roger and I really want to buy a house as soon as possible, and it'll happen faster if I'm working. Roger's dad would help us, but we'd like to do it ourselves. Well, to be honest, it's mostly me. I like to be independent where Mr. Morgan is concerned. You are never to repeat that.

James . . . I probably should say Jimmy. Roger agreed to call him James, but he can't seem to stay on message. When I remind him that we agreed on James, he's quick to apologize, but ten minutes later, it's "what's little Jimmy doing now?" So, it's likely a lost cause. I know I should just let it go, but Jimmy is just so common. James sounds serious, even regal. Like King James I. There's a reason there is no King Jimmy I. Roger keeps bringing up Jimmy Stewart and Jimmie Foxx, an actor and baseball player, but that's the point. One works at make-believe and the other at a boy's game. I want something much more substantial for James.

So far, we've been lucky. James is healthy, happy, and growing like a weed. He seldom cries, and he's sleeping through the night. I suspect that by the end of summer, he'll be crawling all over the place and getting into everything. I can't wait. Mom says I should be careful what I wish for.

Roger is working with his dad on the farm this summer. He's not thrilled about it, but what can he do? The draft board deferred him during the war because Ernest convinced them that James was vital to keeping the farm running, so he needs to keep up appearances for a while. There were lots of whispers at the time about his dad using his influence to keep him out of the service, and I'm sure there's still some resentment. People forget that he was teaching school, coaching basketball, and working with his father at the time. He was contributing more at home than he could have in the Army.

Asking for a deferment was mostly Ernest's idea. I think Mr. Morgan was looking for a way to keep Roger tied to the farm, however tenuously. When Roger decided to become a teacher, it was the first time he'd ever stood up to his dad. Mr. Morgan hasn't given up though and is looking for a way to keep him involved. Then, when Joe enlisted in the Navy after he graduated from high school, Roger felt stuck.

Of course, Roger never wanted to farm. That's why he went to college. Unless he or Joe takes over, they will have to sell the land eventually. Joe doesn't seem to be interested either. He's going to enroll at Alabama on the GI Bill this fall. He was a corpsman in the Navy and says that he wants to be a doctor.

Roger is hoping to start taking graduate courses in educational administration next summer. He doesn't want to be a history teacher forever. There are only three male teachers at the high school, and Roger figures to have the inside track to replace Principal Lynch when he retires. Eventually, he'd like to be Superintendent of Education for the county schools. I think that he's afraid that being a good teacher isn't enough. It's a long story. Ernest was never an easy man to please.

Lots of local boys have been coming home from the war this spring: George Jeffcoat, Ricky Adams, Jack Nichols. It's beginning to seem like old times again. Of course, their return also serves as a reminder of those who won't be returning. I saw Woody Price's mom at the IGA last week. She gave me a hug, and I could tell she was on the verge of tears. I feel so sorry for her.

I probably should go. James will be awake soon, and I need to start thinking about supper! I miss you. When are you getting home for a visit? Please don't wait until the holidays.

Love,
Mildred

****

"Republicans Capture Congress in Epic Landslide," by Ralph Persons, *The Wiregrass Herald,* Nov. 6, 1946, p. 5.

(SPA) Washington, D.C. In a stinging rebuke to President Harry Truman, Republicans won control of Congress yesterday for the first time since 1932. Republicans took advantage of the struggling post-war economy and Truman's unpopularity to flip fifty-four seats in the House of Representatives and eleven in the Senate. It was clear leading up to the election that the Democrats would suffer losses in the midterm elections, but the scale of the route surprised even seasoned political observers.

Republicans painted the president and his party as incompetent in the face of widespread disruptions in the effort to transition the economy to a peacetime setting. In the wake of former President Roosevelt's untimely death in April 1945, pundits often asked in the face of new challenges, "What would Roosevelt do if he was alive?" During the summer and fall, critics began to ask, "What would Truman do if he was alive?"

At political rallies across the country, partisans carried placards reading, "To err is Truman." In the end, the election was a referendum on the beleaguered president. Truman wasn't on the ballot this time, but voters took their frustrations out on his party.

Looking ahead to 1948, Truman's reelection prospects also took a hit.

Now, the road forward becomes even more treacherous for the president. Republicans have chafed under the New Deal's expansion of government for twelve years. Now that they have captured Congress, expect them to push back. It looks like the country is in for a contentious two years.

****

"Few Surprises in Local Contests," by Jack Holden, *The Wiregrass Herald*, Nov. 6, 1946, p. 1.

Turnout was light throughout Wiregrass County for yesterday's midterm elections. The modest turnout seemed to favor incumbents, as there was little turnover in local offices. Fifth District Congressman Democrat Nathan Jordan beat Republican challenger, William Nelson, handily. The incumbent won his eighth term with 74% of the vote. He did even better in Wiregrass County, capturing 78%.

With one exception, the county commission will return intact. Fred Person of Centerville defeated Jeff Allen for the seat vacated by Tom Mullins. Incumbents Frank Ballard, Royce Smith, and Wallace Jenkins won reelection by solid margins. Board Chairman Ernest Morgan of Grover's Fork ran unopposed.

Morgan said that the tepid turnout wasn't a particular concern. "All politics are local," he said at Democratic Headquarters in Centerville. "I think the low turnout in the county reflects the fact that most folks are happy with local government. They don't like Truman, but that wasn't enough to get them out on a rainy day."

Turn to p. 2 for complete returns.

Turn to p. 2 for complete returns.

****

Joel Stewart, "King Cotton," *Alabama Magazine*, August 2007, pp. 5-6.

I grew up in rural Alabama in the nineteen fifties in a region known as the Wiregrass. We had heard rumors of a New South, but we remained skeptical. What we did know was isolation and poverty, and of course, cotton. Cotton was king.

I can still recall riding through the countryside in August and being blinded by an ocean of white stretching to the horizon. Within days, armies of hired hands would descend on the fields and pick them clean. The hours were long—sunup to sundown—and the pay paltry: 3 cents a pound when cotton prices were low; 4 cents when they were high. The average worker picked about 100 pounds a day. You do the math.

I started picking cotton at twelve years old alongside my best friend, Jimmy Morgan. It was Jimmy's grandfather's cotton, but we suffered like any field hand: ten hours a day in the sweltering heat and humidity of a South Alabama August. It was dusty and repetitive and exhausting. And I was happy to do it. I had a weekly allowance of 25 cents, and what I called "cotton money" sustained me until the pecans began to fall in November. Lucky for me, the government wasn't there to "protect" me. Anyway, once you've dragged a 50-pound sack of cotton for ten hours in 95-degree heat, most things in life seem relatively easy.

We lived in a small town like hundreds of others scattered across the rural South. We measured our size by the number of traffic lights in town, four. A federal highway and a county highway bisected the town, dividing it into quarters. The federal highway and the railroad that ran parallel to it were our links to the outside world. As kids, we would hike over to the highway and count the out-of-state license plates, but we called them tags.

Many towns had a cotton gin, and some had several. We had two gins; both were adjacent to the railroad but on opposite ends of town. Toward sunset on a late summer day, the country roads quickly filled with farmers hauling their white cargo to town. The gin removed the seeds from the cotton and compressed the fiber into compact bales. The bales were loaded onto the next train for their trip to the textile mills that dotted the region. For several weeks around harvest time, I fell asleep to the faint, steady hum of the gins that never stopped.

Cotton was king, but the king could be a tyrant. Planted year after year, cotton degrades the soil, leading to reduced yields. Cotton plants were highly susceptible to pests like boll weevils that could ravage the crop, the harvest was labor-intensive, and cotton prices were volatile. Small farms and sharecroppers were never far from disaster.

In high school, I worked at the local picture show that my dad managed and retired from cotton picking for good. When I was seventeen, we moved to Atlanta and I discovered the New South. It wasn't a myth after all. Just slow to arrive in some places.

Several years later, I was driving through the Wiregrass on my way to Panama City and was astonished by the change. Where I expected to see fields of white, there was green—the familiar cotton replaced by peanut vines snaking across the reddish soil. King Cotton was dead, and I had missed the obituary. In retrospect, the tyrant was on life-support even when I was growing up, but I was too young to recognize the symptoms right in front of me.

By 1950, cotton cultivation in South Alabama was a habit. A bad one too. This isn't a eulogy for the King. He needed to go. But I can't say that I didn't learn some valuable lessons under his rule.

Joel Stewart, former City Editor at the *Birmingham Star-Ledger*, is a contributing editor for *Alabama Magazine* and the author of *Crimson Voices: An Oral History of Alabama Football.* He grew up in Grover's Fork, Alabama, surrounded by cotton fields.

CHAPTER 2
BABIES ARE US

"Births on the Rise," *The Wiregrass Herald*," Jan. 6, 1947,
p. 6.

New births in Wiregrass County jumped an unprecedented 35% in 1946, local health officials announced yesterday. Dr. John Franklin of Wiregrass County Hospital said that 1946 started out slowly, but births seemed to double every month. "We expected some increase with the end of the war, but frankly, we've been surprised at the pace," he said. "I doubt that it continues though. But if it does, we're going to need some new schools in a few years."

Local statistics mirror those for the nation. New births nationally jumped from 2.8 million in 1945 to 3.5 million in 1946, a rise of 25%.

****

January 11, 1947

Dear Janet,

It was such a treat seeing you at Christmas. I know that you love life in Montgomery, but I miss you terribly. I never imagined that my best friend would become my pen pal. But you're right to chase your dream. Sometimes, I often felt like I sold myself short coming back here and settling into a familiar routine. I just didn't have the courage to jump into the deep end of the pool.

I remember the day that we declared majors. I was so proud of you for following your heart and picking journalism, knowing that you'd face lots of hurdles. At least I can share your journey, even if vicariously. Not that covering society weddings and debutante balls is my idea of adventure, but you've got your foot in the door.

James and I "read" the picture book that you gave him every night before bed. His favorite animal is the giraffe. Bless his heart; he's trying so hard to talk. He'll babble for a minute and then give me the biggest smile. The other night I told Roger that he was trying to say, "I love you, Mommy." For some reason, that set Roger off. He said that I was spoiling Jimmy. Yes, Jimmy. I don't even correct him anymore. Anyway, it seems that I shouldn't pick James up when he cries, or rock him to sleep every night, or cuddle him so much.

That's what feels right to me. I've been reading this new book about raising children. It came out last summer. It's called *The Common Sense Book of Baby and Child Care*, and it's written by a pediatrician named Benjamin Spock. Dr. Spock says that parents should follow common sense when raising babies: Tend to their needs and show them affection.

Of course, that's not how Roger was raised. "Spare the rod, spoil the child." "Children should be seen, not heard." "Don't embarrass the family." That was his reality, and neither he nor Joe could wait to escape. I'm not going to raise James that way.

I was thumbing through a book in the library last week and I found a quotation from Oscar Wilde that could have come from Dr. Spock: "The best way to make children good is to make them happy." That's my goal for James: that he be happy, and of course, healthy.

I miss reading. Mom passed along Taylor Caldwell's *This Side of Innocence* last fall, and I still haven't opened it. I know, I know: Taylor Caldwell? What I covet right now is escapism. By the time I finish the dishes and get James down for the night, I'm ready to collapse. At least librarians don't have tests to grade and lesson plans to draft. I'm not complaining. I can't imagine life without James.

Don't tell anyone, but one is enough. Nobody wants to hear that, but it's true for me. I warned Roger before we got married, but I don't think he took me seriously. His response was, "Nobody has just one." I assured him that they do. He let it drop, but I don't think that I've heard the last of it. James is barely a year old, and I'm already getting questions from all sides: "When are you going to give James a baby brother?" "Or sister?" I just smile and say, "We'll see."

And we will see. So far, so good. Roger isn't very demanding sexually. When we were dating, he was never pushy, but I thought it was because he was such a gentleman. On our wedding night, he seemed almost as clueless as I was; twice a month seems to satisfy him. Since James' birth, I've insisted that he wear a condom, and I chart my cycle religiously.

I must be the only one in Grover's Fork who does though. Everybody else is pregnant. I swear half the girls we graduated with are pregnant. It's like an epidemic. But that means that James will have lots of playmates in a years.

I should close. It's getting late. Roger is already in bed.

Love,
Mildred

****

August 14, 1947

Dear Mildred,

It took three years, but I'm finally free of the society page. Starting this month, I'm covering education and religion. Not what I want, but a step in the right direction anyway. I won't be satisfied until I'm covering politics and government, but even I know that I'm too junior for that. And oh, I'm a woman. I'd be quite the curiosity in the pressroom down at Goat Hill. I can wait my turn though. I say that but what choice do I have, really?

I did meet the governor last week. Big Jim himself in the flesh. Do you remember Dick Hadley from college? His dad is a judge up in North Alabama, and he managed to pull some strings and get Dick a job in the governor's office after graduation. I ran into Dick a couple of weeks ago at a symposium on Robert Penn Warren at Huntingdon College. I was surprised. I didn't remember him as the literary type.

Of course, that's because he wasn't. It turned out that he was there for the political angle. He's actually a fan of Huey Long. I should have expected that the symposium would focus on *All the King's Men* and not Warren's poetry or even his views on southern literature. The book did win the Pulitzer Prize.

We went out for a drink afterward, and he mentioned this reception at the Governor's Mansion for Representative Walker, who's retiring. Did I want to go? What a silly question. Of course, I wanted to go. Even with Dick Hadley. He's cute and sort of fun, but he'll never love anyone more than he loves Dick Hadley.

Governor Folsom is exactly what you'd expect: tall, handsome, and colorful. With the emphasis on colorful. I was surprised that he wasn't kissing all the girls. At least he didn't have the hillbilly band from his campaign playing. With any luck, we've heard the last of them.

I also met an interesting little man there. A freshman legislator from Barbour County, right up the road from you. George Wallace. Do you know any Wallace's? I don't think he's any older than we are, but Dick says that he's going places. I wasn't particularly impressed, but ever since we studied Napoleon in World History, I've been wary of little men with big plans. He spent the evening bobbing and weaving, and he was definitely intense. I tried to imagine him in a Warren novel, but I decided he'd fit better in a Flannery O'Connor story.

How are James and Roger? James must be running you ragged this summer. But I know that you love it. How's the house-hunting going? Frankly, I'm jealous. I don't know if I'll ever be able to afford a house. I saw a new, two-bedroom bungalow advertised in yesterday's paper for $3800. Yikes! That's a fortune for a lowly beat reporter. I love my apartment though. And my landlord. So, I expect I'll be here for a while.

I'd love to get down before school starts, but I'm snowed under learning the new job and all. Right now, I wouldn't count on visiting until Thanksgiving. Maybe you and Roger (and James) could drive up here over Labor Day. You haven't visited since before James was born. Surely, he's old enough to travel now. Please say you'll come.

Bye,
Janet

P.S. I'm enclosing the last piece I wrote for the society page. It's on Minnie Sayre, Zelda Fitzgerald's mother. As you'll see, she is quite interesting, if a bit eccentric.

****

"Minnie Sayre Takes Stock," by Janet Bell, *The Montgomery Observer*, August 7, 1947, p. 12.

Minerva (Minnie) Sayre, one of the matriarchs of Montgomery society and the mother of Zelda Sayre Fitzgerald, the original flapper, has seen it all and then some. The sprightly eighty-seven-year-old shared some of those memories recently at a reception held in her honor at the Capitol Club in downtown Montgomery.

Born into a prominent Kentucky family in 1860, Minnie Machen married Alabama lawyer Anthony D. Sayre in 1884, and they settled in Montgomery. Judge Sayre capped a distinguished career in law and politics with an appointment to the Alabama Supreme Court where he served for twenty-two years. He died in 1931.

Minnie raised five children (a sixth died at eighteen months), the youngest of which, Zelda, married Jazz Age novelist, F. Scott Fitzgerald. Minnie was active in Montgomery society almost from the start. "We tried to set a tone, a standard, for others in the community," she said. "It was never elitist in my opinion, although everyone might not agree."

Minnie has been a longtime advocate for local theater. A gifted performer as a young woman, she turned down an opportunity to join a professional theater company. "Acting wasn't considered a suitable lifestyle for the daughter of a former U.S. Senator," she noted without a trace of irony. She always encouraged her daughters to participate in the arts, and Zelda was an accomplished dancer as a youth.

Ah, Zelda. "She was always a handful," Minnie admitted. "She had it all: pretty, smart, talented. But she was a free spirit. A rebel. Even before she met Scott. So, nothing she did surprised me. Appalled sometimes, but not surprised."

What about Scott? "Oh, I was opposed to it. He was a Yankee and a Papist, although you'd never know it. And he already drank too much. But Zelda was intoxicated with him, if you'll pardon the pun. I think her father was actually happy to see her married and off our hands. And out of Montgomery."

Scott Fitzgerald died in 1940. "I wasn't surprised," Minnie admitted. "The way they lived, you'd think they had a death wish. The death certificate said, 'Heart attack,' but the booze killed him."

Zelda, who suffers from schizophrenia, is confined to Highland Hospital in Asheville, North Carolina. "Such a tragedy," Minnie said before pausing. "Her father often said that I was spoiling her. Maybe I did. She was my baby."

What's next? "I have no idea," Minnie chuckled. "I was raised during the Civil War and Reconstruction. I look around today and can't believe the changes. We took a horse-and-buggy into Louisville back then. Now, we can fly around the world. Only a fool would try to predict what's next."

Prodded to try anyway, she continued: "I do believe that the war changed a lot. Leveled society for one. I don't think people are as apt to follow social arbiters anymore. So, I'm probably a relic. The war also raised expectations for women. They proved their worth. Many feel empowered by their wartime experience. They don't want to go back. We'll see where it leads. I do believe that young women aren't as likely to take no for an answer if you know what I mean. It might take a while, but the seed has been planted."

CHAPTER 3
NEVER A DULL MOMENT

March 12, 1948

Dear Janet,

It's spring break! Yay! I've got a whole week off at home with James. Roger is working with his dad this week, so it'll be just James and me. We are expecting good weather all week, so I hope to get out a lot. Mom doesn't take James out as much as he'd like. He loves being outside and playing in the sand. I just wish he liked taking his bath half as much.

Everybody warns me to expect the worst with a two-year-old, even Dr. Spock, but so far, so good. James has his moments, but they usually pass quickly. Sometimes it does seem like "no" is his favorite word, but maybe that's because he's heard it so much from me. Dr. Spock says to stay calm and not overreact, but if this is the worst it gets, I'm not too worried. Mom says that I was much worse at two and look how well I turned out. I know you're laughing. You can stop now.

Ernest was elected as a delegate to the Democratic National Convention in July. It's in Philadelphia. All he said was, "It's about time." He's been a party fixture in the Wiregrass region for decades. It should be interesting. He rails about Truman all the time. I don't often agree with him, but Roger doesn't like conflict, so I usually keep my opinions to myself.

It seems to me like we're always on the wrong side of history. We were in 1861 and look where that got us. We still haven't recovered. Now, here we are again with the same fight. Likely same outcome. Ernest, who knows better, repeats the same old, discredited bromide about protecting our way of life. I sometimes want to shout, "It's not just 'our' way of life. What about the Colored? We've made it their way of life too. What about it do you think they want to protect?"

But I won't say anything. It wouldn't matter anyway. Roger agrees with me on this, but he'd never speak out; can't embarrass Dad, you know. Plus, he reminds me, "We have to live here." When I'm honest with myself, I have to admit that in some ways people like Roger and me are worse than the bigots. At least they acknowledge their beliefs. Burke was right that this won't turn out well.

On a happier note, we've found a house that we like and can afford. It's over on North Street near the park. It's Joyce Agee's old house. I'm sure you remember it. A two-story Victorian. It has three bedrooms and two baths. We won't know what to do with all the room. Roger plans to use one of the bedrooms for a study. We close on it next week. You'll have to visit and help me decorate. Best of all, there's a big backyard for James to play, and the park is half a block away. Can you tell I'm excited?

I saw in yesterday's paper that Zelda Fitzgerald died in a sanatorium fire in Asheville, and I remembered the article you sent me last summer about her mother. What a horrible way to go. She was locked in her room. I cannot imagine. For all the early privilege and glamour, she and Scott lived tragic lives. So much wasted talent.

We have *The Great Gatsby* in the school library, but it's seldom checked out. Probably just as well. Not everybody in town would think it's appropriate for teenagers. Or adults for that matter. I would try to find a copy of Zelda's novel, but that would never do. We're about to mortgage our future. I need to keep my job. I know, I know: Self-censorship is a coward's mission.

Don't forget, you have to visit soon to see the house. No house-warming present necessary!

Love,
Mildred

****

April 7, 1948

Dear Joe,

I'm sorry that you couldn't get down over spring break, but I understand. Maybe you can come for a couple days after the semester ends. You can stay with us. (Yes, Mildred, James, and me.) We closed on a house over on North Street just across from the park last week. We're moving in this weekend. It's got three bedrooms, so we'll have an extra bedroom for you any time you're interested.

Of course, Mom won't take kindly to you staying here and not out on Morgan Farms Road. Ha. That's my other big news. The County Commission voted to rename County Highway 14 from Grover's Fork to the county line for Dad. Well, for Morgan Farms, but that's Dad. Nobody has said anything, at least not publicly, but it seems a bit unseemly since Dad's the chairman of the commission.

I don't know if I mentioned it, but Dad's going to be a delegate to the National Convention in Philadelphia this summer. Of course, he's counting on me working on the farm again this summer, especially now that he'll be gone for a while. I was hoping to take a

23

couple of graduate courses at Auburn this summer, but I guess that's out. Mildred says that I should refuse, and I should, but . . . Well, you know how he is when he doesn't get his way.

You've always been stronger than I am where he's concerned. I'm not proud of it. He said some pretty harsh things when I took the job at the high school, but I rode it out. I say that, but I'm still spending almost as much time at the farm as I am at school. I think he's still determined to lure me back, but I'm just as determined to resist. I don't want his farm or his life.

How are things in Tuscaloosa? It sounds like this has been a challenging semester for you. Pre-med is a tough curriculum. I know that I would have struggled with all the science courses. In a few weeks, you'll be halfway through undergrad anyway. Counting med school, it's still a long slog, but it's absolutely worth it. You know that I'm proud of you.

Mildred and James send their love. He points at the picture of you that we have on the side table in the living room and says, "Joe." Mildred always corrects him: "Uncle Joe," she says. Maybe he'll figure out the uncle concept by the time it's Dr. Joe. He's such a joy to both of us. We've been lucky: He's healthy and happy and has always reached developmental milestones early. Did you know that he arrived early (by two weeks!) in the first place? And he keeps repeating that pattern: early to crawl, early to walk, and early to talk.

For a while, I was worried because Mildred was raising him from a book. Maybe you've heard of it: It was written by a pediatrician named Spock. Apparently, it's becoming quite popular among new mothers. I was afraid that Mildred was spoiling James, but so far, so good. I shouldn't have worried. Mildred's mother cares for him while we're at school, so he spends almost as much time with her as with us. After raising three children of her own, I doubt that she needs to consult a book for child-raising tips.

Don't spend all your time in the lab and the library. I used to take a few hours on Sunday afternoons and stroll around campus.

Okay, mainly the girls' dorms and the sorority houses. There were never enough girls to go around though. I doubt that's changed much. I was never very suave anyway. I'm lucky that the school district hired Mildred and that so many of my contemporaries/ competition were away in the service. I know, don't sell yourself short. I know my limitations, and I've made peace with them. I think.

Good luck the rest of the way this semester. And try to find a few days to visit this summer.

Yours,
Roger

****

"Truman Bests Dewey in Surprise Upset," by Jack Mildred, *The Wiregrass Herald*, November 3, 1948, p. 1.

(SPA) Washington, D.C. President Harry S Truman overcame long odds to win reelection yesterday over Republican challenger and New York Governor Thomas E. Dewey. Truman captured 49.6% of the popular vote and 303 electoral votes to Dewey's 45.1% and 189.

Dixiecrat candidate and South Carolina Governor Strom Thurmond carried four Deep South states and garnered 39 electoral votes. Running as a spoiler, Thurmond polled only 2.4% of the popular vote nationwide.

Truman, who consistently trailed in the post-convention polls and had been given up for dead, pulled off one of the most stunning political comebacks in U.S. history. The outcome was in doubt throughout the night, and Dewey did not concede until 11:14 this morning.

In a further rebuke to Republicans, the Democrats recaptured both houses of Congress, reversing the gains Republicans made in 1946.

See "Truman," p. 5

****

"Thurmond Carries Alabama," by Lee Holman, *The Wiregrass Herald*, November 3, 1948, p. 1.

South Carolina Governor and Dixiecrat presidential candidate, Strom Thurmond, swept all but one of Alabama's sixty-seven counties in yesterday's election. Thurmond garnered almost 80% of the popular vote to Republican Thomas E. Dewey's 19%. Democratic nominee, President Harry Truman, did not appear on the Alabama ballot because of a technicality.

Overall, the Dixiecrats won four states and nineteen electoral votes but failed in their effort to unseat Truman who won a majority of the electoral votes without the traditional Solid South in his corner. Notably, Truman became the first Democrat to win the White House without carrying Alabama.

See "Thurmond," p. 5

****

November 4, 1948

Dear Janet,

As you'd expect, there's lots of hand wringing locally about the election results. Truman was never very popular around here and less so after his executive order ending segregation in the military. I voted for Dewey but without conviction. Given a choice, I'd have voted for Truman. On one hand, I'm not sure I know what Dewey stands for. On the other, I know exactly what Thurmond stands for.

It'll be interesting to see what Ernest has to say about the results at lunch this Sunday. He had high hopes for Thurmond. Not to win of course, but to deny Truman another term. You'd think that he'd be a bit humbled, but I doubt it. In many ways, the Dixiecrats are the same clique that led the southern people into the abyss a hundred years ago, and they've never shown any remorse. Worse, they haven't learned anything. Segregation is going to be this generation's Lost Cause, and for what?

Roger says that I need to worry about things that I can control, and he's probably right. He's a history teacher and knows that the Civil War was not some noble struggle. He knows the south today is increasingly isolated culturally and politically because of Jim Crow, but he won't say anything. He learned growing up to keep his head down and keep moving. It's who he is. I'm hoping that when his dad is dead and in the ground that it'll free him. Listen to me. That sounds terrible—maybe it is—but I can't help thinking it.

We have lunch with Roger's parents every Sunday after church; Ernest insists on it. By now it's become a tradition. Tradition: Someone else's idea of fun. Anyway, it's the longest two hours of the week for me. Roger's mom is a great cook, but the conversation is not as appetizing. Mostly, it's the world according to Ernest.

I've known Mrs. Morgan for six years, and I swear I've never heard her say more than five or six words at a time. But she listens attentively and nods at the right time. Everyone knows their role, except me of course, if only I'd nod occasionally.

I shouldn't complain. It's only a couple hours a week. Roger is at the farm a lot though. He's there all day, every day in the summer and on the weekend during harvest. He hates it more each year, but Ernest won't let go.

Roger wanted to take a couple of courses this summer at Auburn, but Ernest insisted that he couldn't spare him. He had the Democratic Convention to attend in July and the campaign to attend in the fall. Maybe next year, he promised. Of course, next year will never come if it's left up to Ernest.

Oh, my ,this is quite the rant. Next time, I promise not to mention Ernest.

Love,
Mildred

CHAPTER 4
NEIGHBORS

March 3, 1949

Dear Janet,

Just wanted to write since I'm in such a good mood today. It looks like spring is here to stay and that's always a treat. I took James to the park today, and he found a new playmate: Patty Martin's boy, Joel. I know you remember Patty. She married Joe Stewart from Centerville. They just moved in three houses down a couple of weeks ago. Joel is only a couple months younger than James, so they're perfect for each other. They seem to get along great for three-year-olds anyway. I hope they become friends. I love this neighborhood but it's mostly older folks. Having a playmate just down the block will be nice.

Joe and Patty are running the picture show downtown (mostly Joe). Besides Joel, Patty is six months pregnant. I don't know when Roger and I have been to the movies. We'd like to get out more, but I don't like to ask Mom to babysit since she has James all day during the week. I do remember now it was last fall when we saw *Easter Parade*. That was fun. We do need to get out more.

Spring break is coming up soon. Roger plans to go up to Auburn during the break and see if he can register early for the summer term. If he's already officially committed, maybe he'll find it easier to fend off Ernest.

When I took the job at the school, I hardly knew Roger. He was four years ahead of us in school. That's an eternity at that age. I was flattered when he started paying attention to me. I can't say flirting, since I don't think Roger knows how to flirt. He was older and, I thought, independent and sophisticated too. Boy, was I wrong! The sophistication is a mile wide and an inch deep. Don't get me wrong. That's okay. I'm not exactly Judy Garland.

It's how tethered he still is to Ernest that worries me. All I could see at the time was that he had chosen teaching over farming. I couldn't see that he had spent all his resolve in that single effort. It's like Roger won the battle but lost the war. He got away but not far, and Ernest keeps trying to reel him back in. I didn't see any of this until after we were married. I'm sure that it was there; I was looking elsewhere. I wonder if anyone goes into marriage with her eyes wide open.

In retrospect, I don't know what I was thinking about anything. I never really had a plan of any sort. That's why I ended up back here in the first place., unlike you. Four years of college, and I was literally back where I started sleeping in my old bedroom for God's sake. Even my curfew hadn't changed. How pathetic is that?

The war was still on, and there wasn't much to do in Grover's Fork. Or anybody to do it with. I was lonely and bored., and along came Roger. When you don't have a plan, it's easier to imagine yourself as part of someone else's plan. And Roger had a plan: get married, start a family, save up to buy a house near the park. Live happily ever after. Yes, it was banal, but it was familiar. Cursed is the familiar for it shall occupy your life.

Oh, my God, listen to me. Four paragraphs ago, I was in a good mood. What happened? You don't need this. I'm going to start over tomorrow.

****

August 6, 1949

Dear Mildred,

God. The Dog Days are here, but I'm the one barking. August was always my least favorite month of the year. I find myself going to the movies just to sit in the air-conditioning. Seeing a good film is a bonus. I think that it's even hotter in cities. More of everything—people, cars, asphalt—but trees.

To answer the question from your last letter: Don't nag. You are beginning to sound like my mom. She can't imagine that I'm single and happy. She writes every time one of the old gang gets married or has a baby. She tries to be subtle, but I can read the despair between the lines. Believe me, I'm not trying to stay single. But I'm not lowering my standards to please her or anyone.

The men at the paper are either married or single for a reason. Usually, a very good reason. I'm not the most popular reporter in the newsroom. It wouldn't be so bad if I weren't unapologetically ambitious. That's apparently not a good look for a woman. Even those who are civil see me as a competitor. The others see me as a threat. Not exactly fertile ground for romance. I should get out more, but the older I get, the harder it is to make the effort. Guys can change their shirts after work and off they go. We women are expected to spend an hour getting ready. After a long day, it's a bridge too far.

So, we'll see. There's so much I want to see and do. It's not just a silly dream. Other women have done it. Martha Gellhorn has done it. Brilliantly. Of course, she faced obstacles. She just had to be more resourceful than the boys. That's how she made it to shore at Normandy on D-Day, and Hemingway didn't. I'm sure that Papa didn't respond well to being bested by the little lady.

I remember reading her reporting in *Collier's* and *Saturday Evening Post* and thinking, *I want to do that*. I know that I have to pay my dues, but I'm not going to cover society, education, and religion forever. I'm willing to sacrifice some things to get where I want to go. What was it Napoleon said about women: Marriage is their whole destination? Well, not anymore.

I just finished a story about the Air Force's graduate school. It's called Air University and it's headquartered here at Maxwell Air Force Base. It's not exactly my beat, but it is education, right? So, I pitched the idea to my editor, and he agreed.

I was attracted to the story because of the Cold War angle, but I couldn't say that. That's certainly not my beat. So, I framed it as an education story. It's not quite the same as hiding out in the bathroom on a troopship to get to Normandy, but it is resourceful. The boys are not going to be happy. Especially when they realize that I've scooped them. I'll send you the clipping when it runs. Let me know what you think.

Roger's summer classes should be over soon. Sunday dinners at the Morgan's must be tense this summer. I'm still surprised that Roger managed to pull it off. Mr. Morgan must be going soft. Ha.

James must be growing like a weed in this summer heat. I miss him more the older he gets. Don't let him forget "Aunt" Janet.

I'm going to try to get down for Labor Day. I've got a book for you: *Other Voices, Other Rooms* by Truman Capote. You've probably heard of it. It was on the *New York Times* bestseller list last year. Dick Hadley, of all people, recommended it.

Capote lived for a time in Monroeville as a child, and the novel is apparently semi-autobiographical. The main character is a precocious and effeminate boy, and that would certainly fit Capote. Wait until you see the photograph of him on the book jacket. It's already stirred up controversy in literary circles. The novel is strange, and some will find it shocking. But I don't mind being shocked. I usually end up learning something.

I should get moving. I haven't picked up the apartment in a week. Lucky I don't have any visitors.

Hope to see you soon,
Janet

****

"Studying War: Air University Prepares Leaders for Tomorrow," by Janet Bell, *The Montgomery Observer*, August 10, 1949, p. B1.

"The Cold War is here to stay." That's the message from Air Force Major General Benjamin Allen, the commandant of Air University, the Air Force's postgraduate school. Headquartered at Maxwell Air Force Base on the western edge of Montgomery, Air University houses the Air Command and Staff College and the Air War College.

Aerial flight in Montgomery dates back to 1910 when the Wright Brothers opened a flight school on the present site of Maxwell AFB. During World War I, the Army operated a repair depot on the site, and between the wars, moved the Army Air Corps Tactical School to Maxwell. Following World War II, the Tactical School moved to Texas, and Air University was established.

The Air Command and Staff College is designed to prepare young field-grade officers for staff duty at squadron and wing level, while the Air War College educates the next generation of senior officers. The yearlong curriculum of the Air War College focuses on national security studies and military strategy, and graduates receive a Master of Strategic Studies degree.

Col. Richard Deal teaches national security studies at the War College. Deal, a decorated fighter ace, echoes Allen's assessment of the future. "We're locked in a long-term struggle with the Soviet Union over the future arc of history," he explains. "The two systems are fundamentally different, and the Communists appear determined to spread their worldview. The key question, which I think the president has already answered, is, 'Does this represent an existential threat to the west?'"

The Truman Doctrine, the Marshall Plan, and the Berlin Airlift point clearly to an affirmative answer to that question. Deal says that the challenge for the nation is to find ways to counter the Soviet threat without triggering World War III. "We might settle on a single overarching policy to contain the Soviets, but we will need to be creative and adaptive in executing that policy. One of our goals at the War College is to prepare future leaders for such a challenge. Air power will be one of the cornerstones of any national security strategy, and some of our graduates will be at the table when that strategy is being discussed."

Gen. Allen graciously agreed to give us unlimited access to two of the War College's officer-students: Lt. Col. Alan Bates and Col. Carter Black. We were able to spend a full day with each, even sitting in on their classes. Both saw extensive combat in the war, Bates flying with the Eighth Air Force and Black flying with the VIII Bomber Command, the predecessor to the Mighty Eighth.

See "War College," p. B2

****

Joel Stewart, "Me & James," *Alabama Magazine*, September 2007, pp. 7-8.

James and I were born only months apart in 1946 in a remote corner of the Alabama Wiregrass. From the time I was three, we grew up on the same block in a small town that differed little from thousands of others scattered across the rural south.

Ours wasn't a particularly prosperous town. We were mostly hard-working, God-fearing people who expected our reward in Heaven. I assume that included black and white alike. Those were Jim Crow years, and the races didn't interact much, especially the young. They had different schools, different playgrounds, and different churches, although the same God, I think. I once asked my mom that exact question. "Of course," she said. "Why would you ask?" I let it go, but I couldn't help wondering if Heaven was segregated. Now, I know: There is no Heaven. Only hell on Earth for many.

I can't remember when James wasn't my best friend. He was an only child, a rarity at the time. His parents were both college-educated. His dad taught history at the high school, and his mom was the librarian. That made James different, but what really set him apart was his grandfather. His grandfather operated the county's largest farm; owned some of the choicest real estate in town, including the picture show that my dad managed. He also ran the County Commission.

James' grandparents lived south of town, but we'd often see him around in his battered GMC truck. James called it the "Georgia Milk Cow." GMC, get it? Occasionally, he drove a black Cadillac Coup de Ville with extended tailfins and enough chrome to make you blink on a bright day. Cadillac was the very symbol of small-town prosperity in the post-war era. James' parents had a Plymouth Sedan. My dad drove a Ford coupe. He always said that Ford stood for Fix Or Repair Daily. No matter, he was loyal to Ford to the end.

James and I attended the same school: From Dick, Jane, and Spot to dangling participles and algebraic equations. James was smart. I was smarter, or maybe I worked harder. There was more pressure on James to do well since his parents worked at the school. Later, after his dad disappeared, he rebelled a bit, but never anything serious.

Wiregrass County School consisted of three schools on a single campus: an elementary school, a junior high, and the senior high. So, I usually caught a ride to school with the Morgans. It was only half a mile to the school, and as we got older, we often rode our bikes when the weather was good. In elementary school, there were three sections of every grade, but somehow James and I always ended up in the same class. It was an open secret among us that James' mom pulled strings to keep us together.

James got a car from his grandfather when we were in tenth grade. His mom wasn't very happy about it, but she let him keep it. It was a brand-new 1962 red Volkswagen Beetle. His grandfather went all the way to Montgomery to get it. You just didn't see many of them in the Wiregrass back then. We went everywhere in that car. We also double-dated in that car, which was great for me in the cramped backseat. It was hard not to get cozy back there.

And then on a hot, still, and cloudless day in July 1963, my life was upended. James had been as much a part of my life as anyone, parents and siblings included, for thirteen years. Then, he wasn't. I knew that the picture show was struggling. Attendance, especially on weeknights, had been falling since television stations started popping up in the region in the mid-1950s. People still showed up on Friday and Saturday nights and for weekend matinees, but fewer and fewer turned up during the week.

Dad always said that he made his expenses on the weekend and his profits during the week. He closed the theater for good on Sunday, June 30. The last picture show in Grover's Fork was *Splendor in the Grass*, a bittersweet drama starring Natalie Wood and Warren Beatty in his debut. I think it was a fitting finale.

James and I went together. We didn't have dates. It felt like a wake. We both loved movies and had seen hundreds together over the years. Before television, books and movies were what connected small towns like Grover's Fork to the world. We already had to drive a dozen miles to find a bookstore. Now, we'd have to drive at least as far to see a movie. We should have seen it coming, but we were kids. Progress in the late twentieth century would not be kind to rural, small-town America.

Dad landed on his feet, finding a job managing a theater in Atlanta, Georgia. I was distraught. Atlanta didn't represent opportunity for me. It represented upheaval.

"There's so much more to do there," Mom said.

"There's plenty to do here," I responded, although I had often complained about how boring Grover's Fork was.

"You'll make new friends," she tried.

"I want my old friends," I whined. I didn't mention Grace, my on-again, off-again girlfriend. I believe that we were off-again at the moment.

The fact is, I wasn't sure that I'd make new friends in Atlanta. I'd never before had to make new friends. I'd had the same friends for as long as I could remember. I figured Atlanta schools would be much larger. What if I couldn't cut it at football or track? What if the girls thought I was a rube?

I was happy and comfortable in Grover's Fork. I wanted to stay. James and his mom said I could live with them. My folks said no, we were a family and families lived together whenever possible. I thought they were being unfair. But I was seventeen and couldn't see things from their perspective.

I cried the day we left. I hadn't cried since we lost in the district finals in Little League when I was twelve. James and I swore that we'd keep in touch, and we did for a few months. I made new friends. It was easier than I imagined. That was a good lesson for the future. I earned a starting spot on the football team, and I started dating a cheerleader. I decided that Atlanta wasn't so bad after all.

Before long, the physical miles were the least of what separated James and me. We had less and less in common. We drifted apart. Change happens. You move on. When I think about James now, I always remember the closing line in that last picture show in Grover's Fork:

"Though nothing can bring back the hour

Of splendor in the grass, of glory in the flower;
Grief not, rather find,
Strength in what remains behind."

Joel Stewart, former City Editor at the *Birmingham Star-Ledger*, is a contributing editor for *Alabama Magazine* and the author of *Crimson Voices: An Oral History of Alabama Football*. He grew up in Grover's Fork, Alabama, surrounded by cotton fields.

CHAPTER 5
A NEW DECADE

"Welcome to the Fifties," *The Wiregrass Herald*, January 1, 1950, p. 4.

We are waking up today to a new year and a new decade. After the past two decades of depression and world war, one can be forgiven for fearing the worst. Turning the calendar to 1930 or 1940 did not usher in happier times. But despite some dark clouds—the growing threat from the Soviet Union, the triumph of the Chinese Communists, and continued economic turmoil in this country—there is reason to hope that the 1950s will be better.

In Western Europe, economies are finally beginning to recover from the war, helped along by the Marshall Plan. And with the success of the Berlin Airlift, the U.S. successfully pushed back against Soviet mischief in central Europe.

At home, despite many false steps, the post-war economy has put down a strong foundation for future prosperity, and in a sign that the average American remains optimistic about the future, births continue to surge. For the fourth year, new births in the United States ranged from 3.5 million to 3.9 million. Wiregrass County Memorial Hospital reported that it experienced the most births ever in 1949.

Wiregrass County Commissioner Ernest Morgan announced last week that tax receipts in the county grew by a solid 5% last year. New businesses are popping up all over the county, and the Alabama Power Company revealed plans in November to begin construction on an electricity-generating plant in the county in 1950.

Morgan, who manages the largest farm by acreage in the county, plans to build a peanut processing plant on property he owns on Morgan Farms Road south of Grover's Fork to take advantage of the burgeoning cultivation of peanuts in the region.

Franklin Roosevelt cautioned Americans during the depths of the Great Depression, "We have nothing to fear but fear itself." While there is still much to fear in the world, there also is much that points to a future of peace and prosperity, so as we look to a new year and a new decade, let's heed the late president's words, roll up our sleeves, and go to work.

****

January 1, 1950

Dear Janet,

Just a quick note to tell you how much we enjoyed seeing you over Christmas. James is playing with the truck you gave him as I'm writing this. He calls it "Aunt Janet's truck." He turns four today. I can hardly believe it. Where does the time go? From Day One, I've heard, "Enjoy every day. It'll pass so quickly." Well, I get it. I'd love to stop time, or at least slow it down some. James is at such a precious age. But wishing and hoping won't make it happen.

Thank you again for the book, I think (first the Capote book, and now this). *Nineteen Eighty-Four* is certainly not the kind of future that I want for James or anyone. Since you know my taste in literature runs toward the rather straightforward realism of someone like Willa Cather, I can only assume that you are trying to broaden my horizons. Well, I'm game for most anything, even for what I thought at first was science fiction, one of my least favorite genres.

I was hooked from the first sentence: "When was the last time your clock struck thirteen?" How can you not be intrigued? Once I started, I couldn't put it down. I'm not saying that I enjoyed it. Orwell's vision of the future is truly terrifying, but I can see its value as a warning against complacency. I passed it on to Roger, and he's almost finished. He's rather adamant that it can't happen here, but I reminded him that the East Germans probably felt the same way before the Soviets took up shop.

Looks like state government won't be as colorful in the next four years. Governor Persons should be more business-like than Big Jim, and that will be a good thing. Ernest isn't impressed. He supported former Governor Sparks in the primary. I'm sure he'll find a way to mend fences though. When our state senator announced his retirement last winter, Ernest could have had the seat if he wanted, but he didn't. He said publicly that he had enough on his plate. The truth is he'd rather be a whale in Wiregrass County than a minnow in Montgomery.

Will you attend Persons' inauguration? Is there any chance that you'll get invited to the inaugural ball? You haven't mentioned Dick Hadley in a while. Is he still around? Actually, you haven't mentioned anyone in a while. I know; don't nag. I just hate to think that you might be lonely. You never even mention any girlfriends either. Don't tell me it's because nobody measures up to me. Ha-ha! The next time you write I insist that you include something exciting that's happened.

Love,
Mildred

****

41

April 1, 1950

Dear Roger,

It's official; I'm a step closer to being a doctor. The acceptance letter from the med school came today. After my interview, I thought that I had a good chance to get in, but you never know. I couldn't open the letter when it came. You would think that after waiting so long, I'd rip it open. But for some reason, probably fear, I was paralyzed. So, I dropped it on my desk and went for a long walk.

I don't know what I thought would happen, but the envelope was still there when I got back. I felt silly. The verdict wasn't going to change no matter how long I put it off. Even so, I'm glad that the news was in the first sentence. I was nauseous just getting that far. And to think that I'm a gnarly combat vet—not so gnarly, I guess.

Now, I've got to buckle down and finish the semester. Then, I'll try to relax a bit this summer. I know that there won't be much relaxing once classes start this fall. I'm not complaining. I'm looking forward to it. I'm not sure how I'm going to work out the finances yet. I'll have used up my GI Bill benefits after this semester. But I'll figure it out. I won't be beholden to Dad. I know that you'd help, but no. You have a family to provide for, a mortgage for God's sake, and your own continuing education. I love you, but don't even think about it.

Pass the news on to Mom; she'll want to know.

I'll need to work this summer, but I promise to get down for a while after graduation.

Love,
Joe

****

"UN Authorizes Action; Truman Orders U.S. Forces to Korea," by Jay Givens, *The Wiregrass Herald*, June 28, 1950, p. 1.

(SPA) Washington, D.C. The United Nations Security Council voted unanimously yesterday to recommend that member states supply military assistance to the Republic of Korea. This follows the Security Council's adoption of Resolution #82 on June 25 condemning North Korea's invasion of South Korea.

Following the Security Council's action, President Harry S. Truman ordered the military to begin preparations to assist the beleaguered South Koreans. North Korean troops are already threatening Seoul, the South's capital, and rumors suggest that South Korean President Syngman Rhee is preparing to evacuate the government.

The surprise North Korean attack on June 25 caught the South Korean troops stationed along the 38th Parallel that divides the two countries by surprise, and reinforcements have been slow to arrive. Pentagon officials privately acknowledge that the outlook for the South is clouded.

The White House has confirmed that President Truman has ordered the U.S. Commander in occupied Japan, Gen. Douglas MacArthur, to begin shipping war materiel to the Republic of Korea (ROC) forces, and the Administration is preparing a $12 billion supplemental budget request to support a U.S. initiative.

****

July 15, 1950

Dear Roger,

By the time you get this, I'll be back in the Navy. I can't explain my decision, but it feels like the right thing to do. I'm still in the individual ready reserve, and the Navy can call me back at any time. Who knows whether Korea will get that bad, but I've decided not to wait.

I've been reading reports that none of the services are prepared for this. They'll need people like me who already have the necessary skills. I expect that lots of guys will be involuntarily called back. It's a shame too. Just when many of us are finally adjusting to civilian life. That's the crazy part. I knew from the moment that I heard the news of the invasion that it'd mean war for us. Despite how much I hated it last time, I felt strangely drawn to the prospect. Maybe I need to have my head examined.

I talked to Dean Barnes at the medical school before making my decision. His advice was to wait, but he accepted my decision and promised to save me a spot in a future class. So, I don't have to worry about burning that bridge.

My biggest concern is Mom. It was hard on her before, and I'm afraid it'll be even harder this time. But if it's not me, it'll be someone else and their mom. Keep this to yourself for now. I've got a week before I have to report, and I want to come down and tell her face-to-face.

When I contacted the Navy, they offered to send me to officer candidate school, but that's not how I can help the most. I'm going back the same as I left: a Hospital Corpsman Second Class. I'll need a reorientation course and some PT, but otherwise, I should be good to go. The PT is a concern. Student life has left me soft and lazy. Physically, anyway. I'd like to return to the Marines. I've heard that my old outfit, the 1st Marines, is being reactivated out at San Diego, so we'll see.

It looks like MacArthur will run the war from Japan. We'll see how that goes. The man's ego makes him dangerous. I'm not sure that I ever heard a Marine say anything good about him. But that's way above my pay grade.

I know that this is a shock. It was a shock to me too. But for some reason, I need to do this. We'll talk soon.

Love you brother,
Joe

****

August 11, 1950

Dear Mildred,

I was shocked at the news about Joe. He's done his part. He doesn't have anything to prove. That said, I respect his decision and his sacrifice. We need more people like Joe and fewer like the politicians around this town. Such hypocrites. They go on about the sacrifices of public service, but most of them don't know sacrifice from self-service. I'm talking about the politicians, not the agency rank and file who keep things running.

I must admit that I've thought about trying to get to Korea myself as a war correspondent. Don't be shocked. You know how much I admire women like Martha Gellhorn and Maggie Higgins. Higgins is already in Korea. It might jump-start my career. I've been at the *Observer* for six years, and I'm still covering school board meetings. I'm better than this. I am.

Do you remember the clipping I sent you of my story on the Air War College at Maxwell? Well, last week, I ran into Col. Deal who I had interviewed for the article. I decided that it was an omen. So, I asked his advice about trying to get to Korea. He admitted that he might know someone who would help me get the necessary approval, but he advised against it.

Of course, I wanted to know why. Well, he said that he expected Korea to be a big story, but only in the short term. The big story over the next decade, he said, was right here. Here? In

Montgomery? I was shocked. Not just Montgomery, but all over the South, he explained. Civil Rights. The integration of the armed forces was only the first step. Jim Crow, he insists, is going to be a casualty of the Cold War.

I had never thought of it that way, but it makes sense. The Soviets were already using our treatment of Negroes against us in the competition for hearts and minds around the world. So, things needed to change, and Truman's embrace of civil rights was just the first step. We'll use justice as the rationale, but if it were simply justice, it would have happened long ago.

Col. Deal is not very hopeful that this revolution in racial affairs will be bloodless. Politicians have hijacked the issue before for political gain and likely will again. In that case, we'll be in for a drawn-out fight. And I'm perfectly situated to cover it.

"You don't always have to go looking for opportunity," he told me. "Sometimes it comes to you."

I didn't want to agree with him, but after thinking about it for a while, I've decided that he's right. I'm going to soldier on right here. We hardly cover race relations at the *Observer*, but if Col. Deal is right, we'll have no choice soon enough. So, I'm going to get ready. Quietly.

Actually, I've already begun. I have a meeting on Saturday with E.D. Nixon who's the president of the local chapter of the NAACP. I identified myself as a reporter with the *Observer*, but I'm not interested in a story. Not yet. I'm interested in a relationship. I hope that he is too. You can't tell a story, at least not honestly, without covering both sides.

Wish me luck,
Janet

****

"UN Evacuation from North Korea Complete," by Jerold Hatler, *The Wiregrass Herald,* Dec. 26, 1950, p. 1.

(SPA) Aboard the *USS Greeley* in the Sea of Japan. There is little joy here in the wind-swept and frigid Sea of Japan as the battered X Corps makes its way down the Korean Peninsula to the South and relative safety.

X Corps under the field command of Marine Maj. Gen. Oliver P. Smith was among the lead elements in the UN's push deep into the North following the successful landing at Inchon on September 15. The Allied offensive stalled at Chosin Reservoir in northeast North Korea when X Corps was attacked and encircled by an estimated 120,000 Chinese troops on November 27. The ensuing seventeen-day battle was fought in freezing weather with temperatures dropping as low as -36.

X Corps reached the port of Hungnam in mid-December where it was met by a 193-ship armada assembled to carry them to safety. The final ship departed Hungham on December 24, and the first Chinese unit entered the port on December 25.

Senior officers aboard the *Greeley* compared the breakout from Chosin and subsequent rescue at Hungnam to the Dunkirk evacuation in the Second World War. One reporter is calling it "The Christmas Miracle." But most of the Marines I've talked with wouldn't agree. While they're happy to be alive, Chosin and its aftermath don't feel like success to them.

X Corps suffered heavy casualties with estimates reaching as high as 10,000. Senior officers say that they expect almost as many weather-related casualties when the final tally is reported. Marine Corpsman Joe Morgan of Grover's Fork, Alabama, said that he had treated as many frostbite injuries as wounds. "I'm from southern Alabama," Morgan continued, "I've never seen anything like it. There really are no words for how miserable it was."

See "Korea," p. 5

****

THE SECRETARY OF THE NAVY
WASHINGTON

The President of the United States takes pride in presenting the NAVY CROSS posthumously to

Hospital Corpsman Second Class Joseph B. Morgan
United States Navy
for service in the following:

For extraordinary heroism while serving with Company A, Third Battalion, Seventh Marines, First Marine Division (Reinforced), in action against enemy forces in Korea on September 2, 1951. Advancing against determined resistance from units of the Korean People's Army (PDA), Company A seized the southeast corner of Hill 602 and established a defensive perimeter. Over the next several hours, the PDA launched several company-size attacks against the Marine position. Hospital Corpsman Second Class (HM2) Morgan repeatedly exposed himself to enemy fire to reach and treat wounded Marines. Despite suffering shrapnel wounds from mortar fire, HM2 Morgan continued to move along the line, administering aid. At one point, HM2 Morgan advanced fifty yards under withering small arms fire to reach a grievously wounded Marine. While attending this Marine, HM2 Morgan was mortally wounded. HM2 Morgan's intrepid actions not only saved Marine lives but also contributed materially to the Marines successful defense of their position. HM2 Morgan's selfless actions reflected the finest traditions of the Naval Service. He gallantly gave his life for his country.

For the President,
Dan A. Kimball, Secretary of the Navy

****

September 9, 1951

My Dearest Mildred,

I can't begin to tell you how heartbroken I was to learn of Joe's death. He was such a dear boy and destined to do great things. It's a damn shame. I know this has been extremely difficult for Roger and you. Do you have any idea yet when Joe's body will reach Centerville? I want to be there for the service. In the meantime, please let me know if there's anything I can do.

Love,
Janet

****

October 11, 1951

Dear Janet,

Forgive me for not writing sooner, but things have been somber here since Joe's funeral. It was a blessing having you here for the service. I usually have Roger to lean on, but this has devastated him. He doesn't have the strength to even pretend to be strong. I try to comfort him, but he's inconsolable. I worry that he'll do something rash. I know, Roger? But I've never seen him like this. James can't even seem to get through the gloom.

I think that James understands what's happened. We explained that Uncle Joe had to go away to Heaven, and that he was happy there. We were going to be honest with James. But how do you explain death to a five-year-old? For now, this seems as good a version as any. I just wish that I knew what to say to Roger. Nothing really prepares us for things like this.

It felt sacrilegious, but I kept thinking of Emily Dickinson's poem "I heard a Fly buzz—when I died" at the funeral service. Do you remember how Dr. Smith tried to make the fly a metaphor for Satan? I always thought that Miss Emily used it because of how ordinary it is. The dying, in that sense, don't hear trumpets or see God; they hear the ordinary all around them. I wonder what Joe heard.

I checked Willa Cather's *One of Ours* out of the library last week, and I'm reading it again. I actually did a research paper on it at Birmingham Southern. Despite the criticism of Papa Hemingway, I found it quite moving. It was exactly what you'd expect from Hemingway: What could the little lady know about combat? In some ways, Joe's experience reminds me of Cather's hero, Claude Wheeler. Claude was sort of a lost soul, and I don't think Joe was, but something led him to volunteer for Korea. We'll probably never know what it was. I think that's what bothers Roger the most. He keeps asking, "Why?"

I know that I won't find the answer in *One of Ours*. I remember my dad poking fun at me for reading so much growing up. "You can't live in those books," he'd say. "You've got to live in the world." He wasn't all wrong. Back then, I often escaped into books. But even when hiding out inside the covers, I discovered useful things. Listen to me; spoken like a true librarian.

Mrs. Morgan seems as lost as Roger, if that's possible. It's hard to get a read on Ernest. Just because he doesn't grieve openly doesn't mean he doesn't grieve. Some men are that way. In all the time I've known Ernest, I've never seen him show any real emotion. He'll feign disgust or even contempt for something or someone, but even that doesn't seem genuine. I want to be fair, but I have no doubt that he abused Roger and Joe. Not physically, although he didn't spare the rod, but emotionally. Nothing either of them did was ever good enough. It left its mark too. And he's still at it. More subtly now, but no less hurtful.

I try to imagine losing James, but I can't. I also can't make sense of Korea. Why is it so important that young men like Joe have to die? Are we going to be safer when this is over? What does your friend Col. Deal say about this? Is communism such a threat to us? People like Senator McCarthy seem to think that they're everywhere. I know that since the Soviets got the bomb, people are afraid, and when people are afraid, they're more credulous. I don't want demagogues frightening us into a war that James has to fight.

Sorry, I'll climb down from my soapbox. Joe's death has made all of us a bit crazy. I just hope Roger can work his way through his grief. James needs a father. I need a husband.

Please come for Thanksgiving if you can.

Love,
Mildred

CHAPTER 6
SCHOOL DAYS

March 4, 1952

Dear Mildred,

I do hope that things are better there. Just the arrival of spring should help. I always find that things look more promising in the spring than winter. Just like things always look better in the morning. Must have something to do with the light or in the case of spring, the longer days.

With spring break just around the corner, you must be busy planning activities to share with James. Just think: This time next year, James will be in school too. I can hardly believe it. Seems like just yesterday that he was a toddler. Perspective is funny, isn't it? When we were growing up, it seemed to take forever. Now that we're the grownups, the speed limit has been raised. Our parents probably feel like they're riding one of Einstein's beams of light.

Did you see in the paper that the University of Tennessee admitted its first Negro student in January? I wouldn't be surprised if something similar doesn't happen at Alabama soon. Mr. Nixon of the local NAACP hinted as much the last time I saw him.

I think that the NAACP has given up on getting much help from Congress because of the filibuster threat and is focusing on the courts instead. It looks like they're going to target education. On one hand, that certainly makes sense. Jim Crow hinges on the Supreme Court doctrine of "separate but equal," and it's hard to defend segregated schools as equal. On the other hand, I wonder if it's a good idea to put the children on the front lines in this struggle. Smart maybe since people are more likely to sympathize with them, but I still wonder. I just hope that our political leaders show better judgment than they did in 1861.

I haven't pitched any stories on the issue to my editor yet, but I'm looking and listening. I'm already getting a reputation as the newsroom radical, so I need to tread softly for now. I can see you laughing. Me, a radical? That just tells you how retrograde most of my colleagues are.

Okay. That's not fair. It's not that they support the status quo, it's that they fear what might come next. I'd call it the "better the devil we know" mindset. They like their jobs, their neighborhoods, and their children's schools. How does integration change all that? Change is always most appealing to those who have the most to gain or the least to lose. For everybody else, it's scary. I understand that. But change is coming.

Have you read anything interesting lately? I've been working my way through Gunnar Myrdal's *An American Dilemma* as part of my education in civil rights. It came out during the war, but I was hardly aware of it until Mr. Nixon suggested I check it out. It's "only" 1500 pages but it's eye-opening. I'm certainly learning things that I didn't know. I'm determined to finish it. Unlike *War and Peace.* Sorry Leo.

My landlord passed on his copy of *The Catcher in the Rye*, which I read while taking a break from Myrdal. I must have looked surprised because he quickly explained that his son had been reading it over Christmas break and left it behind when he returned to school. He said that it was "interesting." It didn't sound like an endorsement. I can see why though. It's too irreverent for anybody over thirty. In that case, you need to read it in the next couple of months. Ha!

Let me know if you can visit over spring break. I'd love to see you, James, and Roger.

Love,
Janet

****

September 3, 1952

Dear Janet,

I just couldn't wait to write you about James' first day at school. There was so much excitement last night that I never found the time. So, I'm taking a break from cataloging books to write. His teacher is Miss Wiggins. You don't know her. She joined us two years ago. She's a graduate of Huntingdon College and is from Elba. She is really good, and as you probably suspect, it's no accident that James is in her class.

He was as excited yesterday morning as I've seen him except on Christmas mornings. He and his buddy Joel rode to school with Roger and me. I didn't pull strings for Joel, but he got Miss Wiggins too, which is good. Neither he nor James would have been as excited for school if they were in separate classes.

I was distracted all day wondering about how he was doing. I shouldn't have bothered; he loved it. He and Joel jabbered all the way home about what they'd done, and James repeated most of it again at dinner. He's already got a crush on Miss Wiggins. I must admit that I'm a bit jealous. But this is part of the natural progression of growing up. Like it or not, he'll never again be as dependent on Mom. Luckily you can't see me now, I'm tearing up.

We're finally seeing the impact of all the births after the war. This year, for the first time, we have three sections of first grade. We had to convert a storage room into a classroom. We'll need to add classrooms if this continues, and I expect that it will.

The next challenge will be finding jobs for all of them. I hope we know what we're doing, but for better or worse, the Class of 1964 will be the pioneers. Let's hope that their journeys will be easier than earlier generations of pioneers. After all, this is my little boy we're talking about.

I had thought that Roger's depression was lifting, but he's slipping again. It started when Ernest roped him into foregoing grad school this summer to help with the business. With the election and all, Ernest swore that he just couldn't keep on top of things without Roger's help. So, Roger lost another summer of courses.

That was bad enough. The new PE teacher and head football coach has made it worse. It's not that he's bad. It's that he's very good. An officer in the war: tall, handsome, and athletic. If that's not enough, he majored in education, but he minored in business. So, he's got the administration block checked. Everybody's impressed, none more than Principal Lynch. Oh, his name is Frank Jackson. He's originally from Phenix City, and he's married, so you can forget that.

Roger hasn't said much, but I know what he's thinking. He's created this entire narrative around football and small-town America. Football is what people care about. They don't care if the chemistry lab has equipment or the library has books. They do care if the football team has helmets and shoulder pads.

If this new coach wins more than he loses, he can write his own ticket. If he wants to move up to the principal's office when Mr. Lynch retires, so be it. Who could make a better principal than the football coach, the ultimate small-town authority figure?

Of course, no one who knows anything about small towns and their football teams would dismiss that possibility, but we don't know what might happen. Coach Jackson could lose more than he wins. After a few years of that, he not only won't be principal, but he also won't be head coach, or he might win a lot more than he loses. Then, he'll be gone to a bigger school and a better job, but right now, Roger can only see the negative. All I can do is keep trying to get through to him and hope for the best. It's wearing me down though.

Listen to me whine. I'm sorry. Thank you for sharing my burdens. I don't deserve you.

How's work? Whine if you need to. I promise to listen.

Love,
Mildred

****

"Ike Wins in Landslide, Stevenson Carries Alabama," by Lee Holman, *The Wiregrass Herald,* November 5, 1952, p. 1.

Former Supreme Allied Commander and Republican presidential nominee, Dwight D. Eisenhower, defeated Democrat Adlai Stevenson in a landslide to become the nation's 34th president. Eisenhower will be the first Republican to occupy the White House since Herbert Hoover in 1933. California Senator Richard M. Nixon will be Vice President. The Republicans also won control of both houses of Congress.

Stevenson, the Governor of Illinois, ran a solid campaign but was handicapped by President Harry S Truman's unpopularity and Eisenhower's reputation as war commander. Eisenhower won every state outside the South and even breached the Solid South by winning Virginia, Tennessee, Florida, and Texas. Stevenson and his running mate, Alabama Senator John J. Sparkman, carried Alabama with 65% of the vote.

See "Vote," p. 4

****

November 8, 1952

Dear Mildred,

It felt strange, but I finally voted for a Republican. Not that it mattered. Even without Sparkman on the ticket, the Democrats were going to win Alabama. I understand the theory of balancing the ticket geographically, but I wonder who thought that putting a confirmed segregationist on the ticket would help. It didn't even seem to help that much in the South. But it didn't matter. Nobody was going to beat Ike.

I'm not sure what to expect from Eisenhower, but I'm actually encouraged. I think that he really means to end the war in Korea, and he has the stature to get it done. Even if it means compromising. Nobody is going to call Ike soft on Communism.

He backed Truman's initiative to desegregate the military, so I'm hopeful that he'll support civil rights reform. He's clearly a moderate, so he'll go slowly, but that's better than not going at all. Whether a gradual approach will be enough to keep a lid on things is the question. So far, the NAACP has been patient. When your strategy is to rely on the courts, you have to be patient. But what happens if their rank and file get tired of waiting?

I asked my editor last week if I could do a story comparing Montgomery's white and Negro schools. He looked like I'd asked to burn down the newsroom. His answer, of course, was "no." But not a forever no. More like a wait-and-see no. We'll cover it when it becomes a story; we won't make it a story. I understand. I really do. But I don't have to like it.

Enough about me. I'm really looking forward to seeing you at Thanksgiving. I hope that Roger is getting better. I'm no psychologist, but from what you say, it sounds like he's suffering from depression. Do you think that he'd consider seeing someone?

Tell James that I want to hear all about first grade.

See you soon,
Janet

****

"The Class of 1964" by Joel Stewart, *Alabama Magazine*, May 2014, pp. 5-6.

Members of the first Baby Boom class, the Class of 1964, began arriving in hospital delivery rooms in the winter of 1945-46— the front edge of a gentle wave that quickly grew into a tsunami. It was only later that demographers would identify the storm and pundits would name it. In the beginning, the Boomers weren't the big story, but peace was.

In the beginning, we didn't seem that much different, except for our sheer numbers. As we slouched toward maturity, a strange thing happened. We looked less and less like our quiet, God-fearing, and pliant parents—the Silent Generation indeed—and more and more like trouble: loud, narcissistic, rebellious. Our parents might have saved the world, but we wanted to change it. That would take more than quiet.

But all that came later. At first, we were just a bunch of anonymous rug rats. In my case, almost completely off the grid in the backwater of rural lower Alabama in a town called Grover's Fork in the heart of cotton country. Home to fewer than 3,000 souls, bisected by a federal highway and a railroad that linked us, however tenuously, to the outside world.

Grover's Fork was a country town and drew its vitality from the surrounding farms. Other than two cotton gins and a peanut processing plant, there was no industry, and retail trade was limited to necessities. There were two schools, one white and one black. Things moved slower at the end of the line.

Wiregrass County School in Grover's Fork included an elementary school, junior high, and high school on a single campus. There was no kindergarten in rural Alabama in the 1950s. Instead, there were backyards, vacant lots, woods, and creeks for playing and exploring, and we were free-range kids. That was an education in itself. To this day, I'm thankful to have missed pre-school and kindergarten.

The school campus included a main building with two wings that hosted elementary and junior high classes. A library and the principal's office completed the main building. There was a cluster of smaller buildings that included high school classrooms, special programs like agriculture, shop, and home economics, and a lunchroom.

The lunchroom was a surplus Army barracks converted to lunchroom duty. Teachers called it the lunchroom. Students called it the slop house. There was no free lunch at Grover's Fork. Everybody either brought their lunch from home or paid 26 cents at the lunchroom. Most of the basic ingredients were government surplus supplied by the Agriculture Department, so in effect, everybody's lunch was subsidized.

The list of what we didn't have was long and varied. There were no foreign language classes unless you counted English. No drivers' education, but we managed to learn. No sex ed. We figured that out too. Some sooner than later. We had a principal but no other administrators. Not to mention no counselors, nurses, or curriculum specialists.

Everybody from grades one to twelve took physical education five days a week. Obesity wasn't an issue. There were four sports teams for boys—football, basketball, baseball, and track & field. Girls had cheerleading. That's it. Title 9 was still a decade away when the Class of 1964 graduated.

The first Boomer class, my class, entered school in September 1952. We were introduced to Dick and Jane and learned to duck and cover in case of a nuclear exchange. Nobody told us that ducking and covering only meant that we'd die under our desk instead of at our desk.

Occasionally, the Cold War would heat up (Sputnik, the Cuban Missile Crisis), and we held our breath until the fever passed. In reality, a nuclear holocaust was too terrible to consider, so we tried not to.

Of course, we discovered rock and roll: Elvis, Buddy Holly, The Beatles. They were loud, raucous, and rebellious. I often wonder which came first, the Boomers or rock and roll. Admittedly, the original rockers were not Boomers, but we made them stars. Just like they helped make us.

And we were the first generation raised in front of a television. Marshall McLuhan famously said later that the medium was the message. He was right. That big box with the small flickering screen was seductive. It also was subversive. We didn't realize that until it was too late.

In 1960 as the Class of 1964 began high school, the country elected John F. Kennedy president. Kennedy was young, handsome, and charismatic, and Boomers embraced him. But the young president would be dead before we graduated, assassinated in November 1963. Things went south from there: LBJ, Vietnam, race riots, and Watergate. Cynicism ensued. Things fell apart. But don't they always?

Joel Stewart, former City Editor at the *Birmingham Star-Ledger*, is a contributing editor for *Alabama Magazine* and the author of *Crimson Voices: An Oral History of Alabama Football.* He grew up in Grover's Fork, Alabama, surrounded by cotton fields.

CHAPTER 7
WRITING TO THE DEAD

February 14, 1953

Dear Mildred,

Happy Valentine's Day! Ha. So, this appears to be my fate: Sitting at home on Valentine's Day and writing to my oldest friend in the world. I guess it could be worse. I could have no friend to write to. Now that I'm thirty, I guess I'm officially an old maid. My mom never uses that term, but I can read it between the lines of her letters. She simply refuses to believe that I'm happy. I'd be happier if I was covering state government, but I'm making progress.

One of my sources inside the local NAACP tipped me off to a lawsuit against the University of Alabama. Apparently, two Negro girls applied to the University last September and were admitted. But once the school discovered their race, it rescinded their admission. With the support of the NAACP, they filed suit against the university. My editor has reluctantly agreed that I can cover the story. Just the facts, he warned. No advocacy. That's fine. Advocacy is for the editorial page. I'll keep you posted. I'm trying to set up interviews in Birmingham with the two young women now.

I know that you gave it to me as a joke, but I actually finished *The Old Man and the Sea*. It was better than I expected. There's still the macho man against nature angle, but the old man of the title is a sympathetic character. Yes, he lands his fish, but fishing seems so much more civilized than tormenting bulls for entertainment.

I'll give Hemingway his due. He can write. But he's not much of a human being in my opinion. I believe that he knows— deep down—that he's a fraud. That's why he tries so hard to appear genuine. And he's fooled lots of people. I wonder if that includes his former wives. Yep, Dr. Bell is in. I made amateur shrinks of all of us.

Does Roger fish? If so, you've never mentioned it. I certainly can't see him hunting. He's too sensitive. Another disappointment for Ernest, I'm sure. Roger seemed happier at Christmas. Or was that a performance for James? It was fun to watch James and his friend Joel play together. They seem as close as brothers. Everybody should be so lucky to have a friend like that. I know that I was. And still am!

I'm going to test our friendship. Do you remember the Valentine's Day when we were in seventh grade and Rodney Adams, who you liked, gave me a valentine? I knew you were upset, so I pretended that I couldn't care less about Rodney or his valentine. Secretly, I was thrilled. I felt guilty for feeling that way when I knew that you were hurt. That's why I've never told you before. Forgive me?

I don't know why Rodney popped into my mind. I haven't thought about him or seventh grade in years. Do you know what he's doing now? He wasn't at our tenth class reunion two years ago. I didn't even notice at the time.

Anyway, I feel better that I got that off my chest. Not that friends shouldn't have secrets. Without secrets, there'd be no friendships. Or happy marriages.

I'm off to bed. Hope Rodney Adams isn't in my dreams.

Love,
Janet

****

July 28, 1953

Dear Joe,

Well, it's finally over. As of yesterday, there is peace on the Korean Peninsula. Well, what seems to count as peace in the Cold War. What was agreed to was an Armistice, not a peace treaty. So, I guess that we are technically still at war. This brave new world of perpetual conflict is not my idea of progress. It's one thing to rail against the Communists. It's another to fight them on their own ground (as you know better than anyone).

I don't know what Ike brought to the negotiations, but it worked; at least he had the mettle to accept reality. I thought that Truman was in over his head. We went to war to defend South Korea against invasion. By the end of September 1950, we had accomplished our goal. The North Koreans had been beaten and pushed back beyond the 38th Parallel. Why not declare victory and come home? I believe that it's called mission creep, and it usually has more to do with ego than strategy. (MacArthur's ego, for sure. But Truman's too.)

It was Truman's call. He was Commander in Chief, and he made the wrong call. In the end, 25,000 American troops died after September 1950. That's three-quarters of the total combat deaths for the war, after we had essentially "won" the war. Why are politicians so careless in assigning young men to their deaths? At least MacArthur got fired, but he's landed on his feet and is still a hero to many. In a post-Hiroshima world, maybe stalemate (isn't that a synonym for containment?) is the best we can hope for. Truman, of course, pays no price at all.

So, after millions of deaths and billions of dollars, we're back where we started: the 38th Parallel. If we've learned anything from all this, maybe it was worth it. I'm not optimistic though. Ike will probably be more circumspect than Truman. He can afford to be. His reputation insulates him from hardline critics. But what happens to future presidents who don't have that armor? No, I don't think we've seen the last of these little adventures.

Well, I just wanted to get that off my chest. I'm not crazy. Yet. I know that I'm not sharing with you. It's just that I don't have anybody else to confide in. Mildred is great, but she shouldn't have to carry my burdens. She's already worried enough about me. Mom's too fragile, and Dad's too judgmental, so little brother, it's you, even if you can't answer.

I hope writing this letter is therapeutic for me. If not, maybe I'll go for a hike and scream at the clouds. Look at me: Writing to the dead and screaming at clouds. If Mildred knew the real me, she'd freak out. So, let's keep her in the dark. James needs one sane parent.

I miss you every day,
Roger

****

December 1, 1953

Dear Janet,

We missed you at Thanksgiving. I forgive you only because you've promised to be here at least a week at Christmas. I almost panicked when I saw in today's paper that it's only "25 Shopping Days Until Christmas." I've hardly started thinking about gifts, much less actually buying them, but I'm excited, especially for James. Of course, he's going to be disappointed. Only second grade and he wants a BB gun, but it's not going to happen, at least not this year. He'll have company though. Joel is also begging for one, and his mom and I have agreed not to give in.

I just hope that Roger cheers up some. I thought he was getting better earlier in the fall, but he's relapsed. It's not just one thing, but the success of the football team hasn't helped. Since we hired Coach Jackson, Roger has seen him as a rival. So, what's good for Coach Jackson is bad for Roger. This fall has been very, very good for Coach Jackson. After a decent season last year (for us anyway), the team won eight of its nine games this fall and the conference championship. It's our first championship since before the war. Coach Jackson, of course, has been anointed a savior.

This is Roger's worst nightmare. He's convinced that Coach Jackson is now the principal-in-waiting. For now, he's probably right, but Mr. Lynch isn't going to retire for years. Anything can happen. Roger refuses to acknowledge that. I wouldn't worry so much, but coming so soon after Joe's death, I'm afraid he'll become overwhelmed. He wants so badly to succeed to prove Ernest wrong. He's a decent man and a good teacher. That should be enough, but he doesn't see it that way.

I'm at my wit's end. I shouldn't tell you, but we haven't had sex since Joe's death. Roger plays with James, but there's something missing. I only hope that James doesn't notice. I know that Roger wants to be a good dad, but his role model was defective. He knows that, but he's not sure how to be the anti-Ernest.

Oh, Janet, I am sorry to burden you with this. If only you had known back in third grade what a burden I'd become, you'd have picked Claire Baker to hang out with. She'd be writing you happy letters from her Mobile mansion. I hate to say, "I told you so," but I was the one who suggested that the caption under her senior picture should be, "Most likely to marry a med student."

Okay, another secret: I was a tad jealous when you were voted "Most likely to succeed." Of course, you deserved it, but a girl can dream. It's quite a burden though. But I know you're going to make it happen, and I won't be the least jealous.

I can't wait to see you at Christmas.

Love,
Mildred

****

"All I Want for Christmas," by Joel Stewart, *Alabama Magazine*, December 2008, p. 7.

Christmas is George Bailey and angels' wings. Bing Crosby and snow. Ralphie Parker and BB guns.

Ralphie Parker? Ralphie, of course, is the 9-year-old protagonist of the classic holiday film, *A Christmas Story*.

Compared to George Bailey's existential quest in *It's A Wonderful Life*, Ralphie's mission is oddly quixotic. He wants one thing and one thing only: "the greatest Christmas present ever." That would be a Red Ryder BB gun. Of course, he's stymied at every turn: "You'll shoot your eye out."

For a kid growing up in the 1950s, Christmas was the best time of the year. The season began on the day after Thanksgiving when the holiday decorations went up downtown and marched slowly, if exquisitely, toward that place where childhood dreams often went to die: under the tree on Christmas morning.

At our house, we didn't wait until the turkey was digested to begin dreaming. No, we began as soon as the annual *Sears Christmas Catalog* landed in our mailbox. For weeks, my younger sister and I kept a daily watch for the mailman, hoping to be the first to hold the sacred book. Mom often said that if we'd spend half as much time with our schoolbooks, we'd be geniuses.

But how could fractions and predicates compete with bicycles, roller skates, and BB guns? In reality, our obsession was the very definition of insanity. Dad ran the local picture show, and Mom helped out when she could. Resources were finite. The standard formula at our house was one impractical present and lots of practical gifts like clothes. That still allowed room for a boy (or girl) to dream.

If we suffered a drought of toys, we enjoyed a surfeit of fruit, nuts, candies, and cakes. Of course, no treat could replace a Daisy Red Ryder BB gun. I started asking for a Red Ryder when I was in second grade. I figured that my parents would say "no" though. My best friend, James, said that our parents were always going to say "no" the first time we asked for anything. It didn't matter if it was ab BB gun, baseball glove, or a car, so ask early and get the "no" over with.

James was a smart kid, but he was wrong about the Red Ryder. My mom's disapproval seemingly knew no bounds. Year after year, she stood firm in her opposition. "They're dangerous," she'd begin. "You'll shoot out a window." And the coup de grace, "Why do you need a BB gun anyway?"

What kind of trick question was that? Even a kid knows that a BB gun has no useful purpose. In desperation, I trotted out the universal lament of the thwarted child, "Everybody has one." Check. To which my mother coyly replied, "You're not everybody." Checkmate.

My mom finally relented the year I turned ten. She didn't say why. I didn't ask. Of course, nothing had really changed. I had no apparent use for a BB gun. The windows were still vulnerable to an errant shot. And in the wrong hands, they could be dangerous. But, of course, that didn't describe me.

Well, before the sun had set on Christmas Day, I turned that Red Ryder on my younger sister and shot her point-blank in the chest. Fortunately, I was far enough away that it didn't even break the skin, and she forgave me. More importantly, she didn't tattle. So I lived another day to do something else foolish.

Many things have changed since that long-ago Christmas. BB guns are out. Smart phones and video games are in. Sears is down and almost out. Amazon is in. The Christmas countdown, like political campaigns, seems endless.

Some things haven't changed. When my own 10-year-old son asked for a BB gun, I said, "They're dangerous. You'll shoot out a window. Why do you need a BB gun anyway?" All true. But irrelevant. A BB gun isn't about practicality. It's a milestone. A rite of passage.

And that's enough. As long as you don't shoot your eye out.

Joel Stewart, former City Editor at the *Birmingham Star-Ledger*, is a contributing editor for *Alabama Magazine* and the author of *Crimson Voices: An Oral History of Alabama Football*. He grew up in Grover's Fork, Alabama, surrounded by cotton fields.

CHAPTER 8
MISSING

"Local Teacher Reported Missing," by Mike Mason, *The Wiregrass Herald*, January 4, 1954, p. 1.

Roger Morgan of Grover's Fork, a popular social studies teacher at Wiregrass County High School, was reported missing by his father, Ernest Morgan, and his wife, Mildred, on Sunday. The senior Morgan is the proprietor of Morgan Farms and the Chairman of the Wiregrass County Commission.

According to Grover's Fork Chief of Police Michael Thomas, Morgan told his wife that he was going to his office at the high school to grade papers for a few hours. Although Mrs. Morgan says that she can't be positive, she believes that her husband left the house around 3:00 p.m. on Saturday. When he didn't return before dark, she contacted her father-in-law who found Morgan's car in the school's parking lot.

No other trace of Morgan was found at the school. Chief Thomas said that there was nothing to indicate a struggle at the school and that Morgan's car was unlocked and the keys were in the ignition when his father found it.

The Grover's Fork police issued a Missing Person's Report Sunday afternoon. The Wiregrass County Sheriff's Office and Alabama State Police have joined the investigation.

Chief Thomas said that there is no evidence at this date of foul play. Mrs. Morgan told police that it didn't appear that any of Morgan's clothes or personal items were missing. Searches of Morgan's home, office, and car turned up no clue as to his disappearance.

Morgan is thirty-two years old, stands 5'11," and weighs 170 pounds. He has short brown hair and green eyes. He was last seen wearing tan corduroy slacks and a blue dress shirt.

Anyone who has seen Morgan or has any information regarding his disappearance is asked to contact the Grover's Fork Police Department (MA 2-4576), the Wiregrass Sheriff's Office (WI 6-7845), or the Alabama State Police (ST 2-8769). The Morgan family is offering a $500 reward for any information leading to a resolution of this case.

****

January 5, 1954

Dearest Mildred,

I was just devastated to hear the news about Roger. I can't even imagine what you must be going through. James, too. If there is anything that I can do, please let me know.

I tried to call today but couldn't get through. Please know that you can call me if you need someone to lean on.

I'm coming down on Saturday. Until then, I'll be praying for all of you.

Love,
Janet

****

February 17, 1954

Dear Janet,

Thank you for everything. You have been a blessing during all this. Everybody has been supportive, but you are the one person that I feel comfortable confiding in. Mom tries to be helpful, but she's so judgmental that I can't really confide in her. To be fair, she's been very good with James. Roger's mom has completely shut down. Not that I blame her. First, Joe, and now Roger. I'm really worried about her.

James has been a revelation. Sometimes, I have to remind myself that he's only eight. Of course, he's sad, scared, and confused, but he's decided that he needs to be strong for me. If only Roger had been as strong.

I say that, but I honestly have no idea what happened to Roger. There have been no credible sightings and no ransom demands. Anyway, Roger had no enemies, at least none that I'm aware of. Ernest has plenty of enemies, but anyone who knows Ernest knows that this isn't the way to hurt him.

I do know that Roger hasn't been happy for a long time. Maybe he finally snapped. I just hope that if that's what happened, he hasn't harmed himself. I keep thinking about Judge Crater. I bet people disappear all the time. Who hasn't, in a rare moment, at least thought about the possibility?

I know that Roger often felt trapped. He never said so in so many words, but it was there between the lines. Maybe he just couldn't see a way forward here. I can understand that. I can't understand leaving James and me in limbo. Neither can I forgive it, if that's the case.

Now that the initial shock has worn off, I've begun to think about a future without Roger. I know that it's morbid, but what can I do? Hide my head in the sand? We'll miss Roger's salary, but we can just about get by on mine. We'll just have to scrimp.

How soon we forget. Scrimping by was a way of life when we grew up, and if push comes to shove, my folks will be able to help out. Ernest not only put up the money for the reward but also offered to pay the mortgage. I hate to be ungrateful, but I will not be indebted to that man. His argument, "Charity begins at home," was tone-deaf and insulting.

James and I are returning to school tomorrow. I think it's the best thing for both of us. The sooner we get back to some semblance of normal, the better. His friend, Joel, has been over a lot during all of this, and it's really helped James. Play is sometimes the most effective antidote for life's disappointments. Anyway, I've talked with his teacher, and she's been very understanding, so I'm hopeful that'll work out.

As for me, I've just got to keep focused on the task at hand. The last thing I need is to break down at school. Principal Lynch insisted that I take as much time as I need, but I don't want to hold James out any longer, and if I'm sending him back, I need to go back too. There's comfort in solidarity. Right now, James needs to know that I've always got his back.

Thank you again for being the best friend a girl could ask for.

Love,
Mildred

****

June 6, 1954

Dear Mildred,

Now that school is out, I do hope that you and James will visit. I'll take a couple of days off, and we can take James to the zoo and to the ballpark to see the Rebels. I'm sure he'd love that. This year's team is affiliated with the Boston Red Sox, and they're pretty good. They have one player in particular who looks like he'll be playing in the big leagues before too long. His name is Albie Pearson, and he's a scrappy little guy, only 5'5" but he plays much bigger. I think that James will like him. I'm sure that we'll find lots of other things to do as well. Please consider it. You can't just sit around the house all summer.

If you've read today's paper, you know that Big Jim won the primary yesterday. It wasn't much of a contest. Despite the scandals of his first term, he's still extremely popular with voters. Given the recent *Brown* decision, he's exactly what we need. I'm hopeful that his moderate views on race and his refusal to demagogue the issue will help the state navigate what's to come. It's perhaps lucky that the Court didn't release its ruling until May 17, and it didn't become an issue in the campaign.

The *Brown* decision threw everybody into a tizzy around the Capitol. Nobody knows exactly what to expect. Yes, the Court ruled that segregation was "inherently unequal" and therefore unconstitutional, but it didn't offer any remedy. So, without a remedy, nothing really changes, right? I imagine the Court will get around to proposing a remedy sooner or later, but who knows?

I talked with a few sources in the Negro community here, and while they are pleased with the decision, they realize that this is the beginning, not the end of their journey. They expect pushback, of course. They remember the 14th and 15th Amendments and the pushback then. What's different this time is that officials of the national government aren't as likely to abandon them this time. I expect the Cold War to do more good at home than abroad. Listen to me: So young and already a cynic.

Okay, maybe not so young. Thirty-two isn't so old though. Of course, I expected to have won at least one Pulitzer by now. I've been at the *Observer* for ten years now. I've paid my dues, and I'm good. The rumor around town is that we're finally getting a television station later this year. Columbus already has two stations. Two! And there's talk of a station going in down in Dothan of all places.

Anyway, our statehouse reporter apparently is among those being considered for the station's news team. He's being quite smug about it. If he leaves, that job should be mine. If it does open up, and I'm passed over, I'm leaving. Why is it that patience is a virtue only for women?

Okay, enough of that. I'm either going to move forward here or somewhere else. Period.

Tell James hello. And come soon!

Love,
Janet

****

September 14, 1954

Dear Janet,

Sorry I haven't written in a while. It's been hectic around here getting back into the routine of work (for me) and school (for James). James is in Mrs. Jones' third-grade class. I love Mrs. Jones, but it's disconcerting when your son has the same third-grade teacher that you had. Remember how old we thought she was? She couldn't have been more than thirty at the time. She must appear ancient to James. He likes her though, so that's good. I know that he's in good hands.

James still talks about our visit this summer. I thought that the zoo would be the highlight of the trip for him, but no, it was the baseball game. He's decided that he wants to be a professional baseball player. How many young boys share that dream? I'm not going to tell him what the odds are that any one of them will make it. Everybody needs to have dreams. I've shifted my dreams to James. I hope that he doesn't realize that though. I don't want to burden him.

I'm amazed at how resilient he seems. He seldom brings up Roger, and when he does, I'm struck by how direct he is. He believes that Roger ran away because he was unhappy. It sounds naïve, but I actually agree. He also thinks that when Roger's happy again, he'll come home. That one I'm not so sure of.

The FBI joined the investigation a couple months ago but has come up empty. They did find that Roger hasn't paid Social Security taxes since he disappeared. That would suggest that, if alive and working, he's using another identity. Or, working off the books somewhere. Otherwise, there's been nothing new. I get the impression that the investigation is losing momentum by the day.

I'm beginning to think that we'll never know. The FBI special agent out of Montgomery who talked to Ernest and me said that thousands of people go missing every year, and not all of them are your typical teenage runaway. Some are eventually found, but many aren't. He advised us not to get our hopes up.

And not knowing is worse than knowing in more ways than one. I got a notice a couple of weeks ago that Roger's life insurance premium was due. Now, that was a shock. As it turns out, we can't collect on the policy because Roger is not "dead," at least not legally. And without evidence of his death, he can't be declared dead for at least seven years, so I have to continue paying the premiums for seven years if I want to collect the insurance when he's finally "dead." I decided to let the policy lapse.

I also discovered that we can't claim Social Security Survivor's benefits for James because his father is not "dead." That extra money would have helped. I understand that rules are rules. But if Roger is dead, we're being denied lawful benefits. I would be more bothered by all this if I really thought he was dead.

My parents have decided that Roger is in Havana working in a casino or nightclub. I can't imagine that. I can imagine him in the Keys working on a fishing boat though. Wherever he is—and I'm assuming he's alive—I bet he's working outside. He enjoyed teaching, but he was happiest when he was outside.

Other than teaching, what he knows is farming, so maybe he's found a job on a farm. That would probably work for someone who's hiding in the open. I try not to dwell on this, but I can't help but wonder where he is. I think that I know the why of his disappearance, but the how and where are mysteries to me. It's hard to ignore a mystery when it's your own life.

On that happy note, I'll sign off.

Love,
Mildred

****

November 1, 1954

Dear Mildred,

How was your Halloween? James is at the age that he probably insists on going out alone. I imagine that he went with Joel, so that's some consolation. I know that I'd be tempted to shadow them to make sure they're safe. But you've got to let go sometime. I know: Easy for me to say.

What about my Halloween? I'm glad you asked. I finally got the treat I wanted. You guessed it. Montgomery's own WHOD-TV is going on air on Christmas Day, and they've hired the *Observer*'s own Bill Carty for their news team. And I'm taking his spot covering state government. FINALLY. The Boss told me yesterday. I must say that I was more relieved than thrilled. I honestly was going to leave if I didn't get it, and I really didn't want to leave.

I think that Col. Deal of the Air War College is right, and civil rights is going to be THE story for several years. How could Alabama—and Montgomery—not be at the heart of the story? I'm torn about this, and I have to admit that I feel vaguely guilty. The best solution for us as a society would be if people accepted the inevitable, even if reluctantly. That would be a story, but not THE story. See my dilemma? What's best for me professionally isn't what's best for society.

I've learned to rationalize that I can't control what happens. I can only cover it to the best of my ability. Thus, I'm off the hook. Isn't it interesting how that works? Anyway, racial integration isn't going to happen without a fight. There's too much fear, not to mention hate, for that to happen and too few leaders willing to tack against the wind. So, a battle is brewing, and if that's good for me as a reporter, it's not my fault. Convinced? Well, neither am I.

With WHOD going on air next month, I guess I'll have to buy a television set. I know a few people who already have them. With an outdoor antenna, they can get remote stations like WBRC from Birmingham. I've seen televisions displayed in department stores, but the screen is so small you have to gather 'round pretty close to see clearly. Lots of people seem hypnotized by them, but I'm going to reserve judgment for now.

You should consider getting one though. Grover's Fork is close enough to receive stations from Montgomery and Columbus. And it looks like a station will be going on air down in Dothan next year that you'll be able to get. During the baseball season, ABC network airs a Saturday afternoon Game of the Week. I bet that James will love that.

I should go. Just wanted to share the big news with you.

Love,
Janet

CHAPTER 9
THE MEDIUM IS THE MESSAGE

March 6, 1955

Dear Mildred,

Do you remember the old Bismarck—well, I think it was Bismarck, although it sounds more like Mark Twain—quote, "Laws are like sausages. It is best not to see them being made"? Well, I can assure you that it's true. At least in the Alabama Statehouse it is. I've only been covering this beat for a few months, but I've seen and heard things that turn my stomach. Most of it doesn't get into the paper.

I've had some "discussions" with my editor over how much information our readers need. You know my position: Give it all to them and let them decide what they need. Of course, I don't have to answer to the paper's owners who sign everybody's check. Funny how that works. I can't complain. Mac is basically on my side and gives me as much freedom as he can. I just have to be resourceful in how I use that freedom.

So far, Big Jim has been better served by the legislature than he was in his first term. It looks like the highway bond issue is going to pass. That'll be a big win for him. Even so, I don't think his political reforms—repealing the poll tax and legislative re-districting have a chance. He'll be lucky to hold the line on racial issues in the wake of the *Brown* decision.

I don't think there's any chance that he'll get his constitutional convention. He regularly calls the Alabama Constitution the worst in the country, but the economic interests that drafted it back in 1901 haven't gone away. Big Jim might have more support in the legislature than he did in his first term, but it's not nearly enough to scrap that relic. Real reform likely depends on the courts, not the legislature.

Speaking of which, I think that we have a case right here in Montgomery that should stir things up. Last week, a 15-year-old Negro girl refused to give up her seat on a city bus and was arrested. The story was covered by the police reporter, but my sources tell me that the NAACP is planning to challenge her arrest on the grounds that segregation of public accommodations is unconstitutional. If the *Brown* decision is followed, that seems to be the only logical conclusion. We live in interesting times.

With spring break coming up, I do hope that you can find time to visit for a couple of days. The Rebels won't start their season for another month, but I'm sure we can find something to occupy James. If we can tear him away from the television. I must admit that it's intoxicating. That's not an endorsement. Instead of reading in the evening, I find myself defaulting to the faint light in the corner. Is that going to be the future for us all?

Don't let me influence your decision about getting a set. It's the new thing. Everybody in the newsroom discusses the programs. The holdouts are seen as squares, if not Luddites. I'm sure that James will be begging for one once his friends have them. You'll be fighting a losing battle. Of course, the next battle will be over how much is enough.

Let me know if you can come.

Love,
Janet

****

June 10, 1955

Dear Janet,

Well, I held out against getting a television at least until the school year ended. James and I picked out a set at Meyer's last week. Bill Lee came out and put up the antenna and connected everything the next day, just in time for James to watch the Game of the Week. It's on CBS this season, and we were able to get it on WRBL out of Columbus. The new station in Dothan, WTVY, is also a CBS affiliate, but we decided that WRBL's signal was clearer. Joel came over and he and James were mesmerized. Imagine watching a professional baseball game in your living room!

I didn't watch the game, but I've sampled quite a lot so far. On Tuesday night, we watched a show called *The $64,000 Question*. It's brand new apparently. If you didn't see it, you should. The setup is kind of hokey, but it's interesting. It's a game show and candidates are put in a soundproof booth and asked questions of increasing difficulty. If they answer each correctly, they proceed to the final question, which is worth $64,000. It's probably about as intellectual as television is going to get. I'm not ashamed to say that I'm hooked. What does that say about me?

James and Joel play baseball almost every day. They can hardly wait until next year when they'll be old enough for Little League. A few of their friends from the neighborhood are playing this year, and we've gone over to the park a couple of times to watch. It's too bad eligibility is based solely on age. James and Joel are both much better than some of the kids who are playing. I guess they have to have rules.

James reads the Sports page every day. I think that's why he was so anxious to learn to read. Whatever works, right? He checks the box scores and the standings religiously. His favorite player is Mickey Mantle who plays centerfield for the New York Yankees, so the Yankees are his favorite team. That's good because the Yankees usually are the best team. Roger used to root for the St. Louis Cardinals because he could listen to their games on the radio when he was growing up.

James also has become a fan of bubble gum. I don't know how much he likes the gum, but he covets the baseball cards that come wrapped with the gum. He desperately wants a Mickey Mantle card, but so far, no luck. Joel likes Pee Wee Reese of the Brooklyn Dodgers; so naturally, he's a Dodger's fan. Fortunately, the Dodgers and Yankees play in separate leagues, so that's not an issue yet. But a Yankees-Dodgers World Series would pit the boys against each other.

I'm sure that you saw the news about the Salk polio vaccine. The county health department is going to be administering the shots at the school starting this fall. It's wonderful news. Bobby Smith, who was in first grade with James, got polio before the year was out. He's still in a wheelchair. The vaccine is too late for him, but it'll save future generations from a scourge.

What's the word around the Statehouse regarding the Court's ruling in *Brown II*? Many of them can't be happy with the order for the states to desegregate their public schools. I'm afraid that I agree with you: It won't happen without a fight.

The Court's timeline seems more than a little vague. What in the world does "with all deliberate speed" mean? It sounds like an oxymoron to me. Speed is fast. Deliberate is slow. If they let the individual states decide what it means, school integration will take a generation.

Now that the Court has ruled in their favor, I don't think the NAACP is going to be happy with anything too deliberate. On the other hand, they've been waiting for ninety years already. I hate it that the schools have to be the battleground for this. The children—of all colors—deserve better.

Nobody talks much about the way forward around here. At least not around me. It's almost as if they've decided that if they ignore it, it'll go away. A few of the teachers have said that they won't teach Negroes. I'm sure that you can mostly guess which ones. And a few loudmouths around town rail about closing the schools if it comes to it. Most folks just keep their heads down and go about their business.

Jack Mildred over at *The Wiregrass Herald* interviewed Wiregrass County School Superintendent Coleman Royce after the *Brown II* ruling was issued, but he dodged the questions about desegregation. Nobody around here paid much attention to school board elections before, but I bet the sleepy old school board is about to be shaken to its foundation.

I feel sorry for Mr. Royce. He genuinely seems interested in the best interests of the kids, and there hasn't been a hint of wrongdoing since he took over fifteen years ago. You can't say the same thing about the County Commission. Ernest has managed to stamp out any brush fires, but there's been plenty of smoke. I think that a lot of these officials hang on so long because they're afraid of what their successors will find.

Oh my! Somebody take away my soapbox. I'm sorry. You deal with this stuff every day. You don't need my stories too.

Next time I promise not to mention politics or politicians.

Love,
Mildred

****

"Montgomery's Negroes Boycott City Buses," by Earl Thomas and Janet Bell, *The Montgomery Observer*, December 6, 1955, p. 1.

Montgomery's buses were operating at an estimated 25% capacity yesterday as the city's Negroes launched a boycott in protest of the bus system's policies of racial segregation. Prompted by the December 1 arrest of Rosa Parks, a seamstress and the secretary of the local branch of the NAACP, for refusing to yield her seat to a white man, the boycott follows a series of recent arrests of Negro riders who resisted orders to vacate their seats.

The most recent such arrest before Parks was 15-year-old Claudette Colvin who was arrested on March 2 of this year. The NAACP has appealed Colvin's conviction.

Parks was found guilty in court yesterday and fined $10 plus court costs of $4. She paid the fine but promptly appealed the verdict.

The Women's Political Council called for a boycott of city buses in a flyer circulated last week. Over the weekend, the local NAACP, under the leadership of E.D. Nixon, endorsed the boycott and formed the Montgomery Improvement Association (MIA) to lead it. The 26-year-old pastor of the Dexter Avenue Baptist Church, the Rev. Martin Luther King, Jr. was selected to lead the effort.

King, who took the helm at Dexter Avenue last year, received his Ph.D. from Boston University in June. A source that attended the meeting setting up the MIA told the *Observer* that while some local ministers expressed reservations about the boycott, King spoke up in favor. For now, he will be the public face of the protest.

Boycott organizers held a mass meeting yesterday evening at the Holt Street Baptist Church where King addressed the crowd. When he asked if the crowd supported continuing the boycott, the response was overwhelmingly positive.

See "Boycott," p. 5

****

December 10, 1955

Dear Mildred,

Just in case you didn't see the recent story on the bus boycott in the *Observer*, I'm sending you a copy. I shared the byline with Earl Thomas who covers local politics, but I did most of the reporting and writing. The time I've spent making connections among the Negro leadership here in Montgomery is finally beginning to pay off.

I wish that I knew Rev. King better. He's been in town about a year, and I've only met him a couple of times. He's awfully young to take this on, but E.D. Nixon seems to think that he can handle it. He is impressive. He's smart—he has a doctorate from Boston University—and articulate. It's going to get bumpy soon enough. Between the *Brown* decision and this, the mood among many whites has darkened considerably. I hope that we get through this without any violence, but I wouldn't bet on it. And this is the Christmas season. So much for goodwill toward men.

That reminds me: I've been reading Flannery O'Connor's short story collection, *A Good Man Is Hard to Find*. In a word, it's pretty dark. Okay, that's two words. So, shoot me. Anyway, the title story is about a serial killer for whom murder is as ordinary as sweat in the summertime. Don't expect a happy ending. O'Connor is an interesting writer, but I'm not sure that southern gothic is my style. Don't rush out and buy it. I'll bring you my copy at Christmas.

I've found that I prefer short story collections to novels. With my schedule, novels take forever. And no, I can't blame my languor entirely on work. I also need my television fix occasionally. With short stories, time isn't a concern. I can finish what I start in an evening, and it doesn't matter how long it is before I get back to the book.

Speaking of Christmas: What can I get for James? What books does he like? What about Erector sets? Just give me some suggestions, and I'll take it from there.

See you soon,
Janet

****

December 14, 1955

Dear Janet,

Yes, I read your piece on the bus boycott. I thought it was very good. Will you be covering the story going forward? Just be careful. I imagine that emotions are running high on both sides.

James has a basic Erector set, but I'm sure he'd like a more advanced set. Mrs. Newsom, his fourth-grade teacher, has been reading to the class every day after lunch. One chapter every day. In November, she read *The Tower Treasure*, the first of the Hardy Boys' series. James loved it. He insisted that I buy the second volume, *The House on the Cliff*, which he devoured. Why don't you get him one for Christmas? The third volume is titled *The Secret of the Old Mill*.

I never read any of the *Hardy Boys* books, but we were in thrall to Nancy Drew. If I'm not mistaken, we were about the same age as James is when we discovered Nancy. For a while, I wanted to be Nancy Drew so badly. Of course, you were more the Nancy Drew type, then and now. You were more independent and self-confident. I also wanted to be more like you. (Surely you knew that.) A confession: In a way, I still do.

James went with me to pick out your present last Saturday. He's pretty excited about it. He and Joel picked up pecans all over town to make some extra money for Christmas presents. He wanted it to be his money, not money I gave him. I'm pretty proud of him.

See you soooooooon.
Mildred

****

"The Hardy Boys," by Joel Stewart, *Alabama Magazine*, January 2008, pp. 11-13.

Fourth grade was mostly the pits. To begin with, I was sure that my teacher, Mrs. Newsom, was a real-life witch. With broomstick and all. Hidden away in the coatroom. It didn't help that she had favorites—teachers' pets we called them. That particular menagerie did not include me. But I digress.

The only good thing that I remember from fourth grade is the Hardy Boys. Before fourth grade, we laid our heads on our desks after lunch and rested, whether we were tired or not. I figured out later that it was the teachers who really needed a break, not us. In fourth grade, that tradition ended. Instead, Mrs. Newsom read us a chapter from a novel each day after lunch. Sometimes, if the story was particularly exciting, we pleaded for a second chapter. Sometimes, she agreed.

As luck would have it, one of the books that Mrs. Newsom read to us was *The Tower Treasure* by Franklin W. Dixon. It chronicled the adventures (and misadventures) of two teenage detectives—sleuths, the author called them—and I was hooked from chapter one. So was my best friend, James Morgan, and when we discovered that there was a whole series of Hardy Boys mysteries, we begged our mothers for more.

Frank and Joe, the Hardy Boys, were the sons of a world-famous detective, who often allowed his precocious sons to help with his cases. They lived in Bayport, a fictional city on the East

Coast, and had everything a young boy could dream of having: a roadster, twin motorcycles, a speedboat, pretty girlfriends, and more freedom than I could imagine.

They were always on the go: tracking down hidden treasure; exploring caves, tunnels, and deserted coastal islands; stumbling upon secret passages and trap doors; and outwitting a host of pirates, smugglers, counterfeiters, and thieves.

In their spare time, they were honor students and star athletes.

How could these fictional sleuths not seduce an impressionable young boy? Especially one stuck in an isolated outback where roadsters, motorbikes, and speedboats, not to mention adventure, were in short supply and curfews were strict, at sundown.

I identified with Frank, the older brother, because he was more serious and had dark hair. James liked Joe who was blond and less serious, though James had brown hair and was relatively intense. Maybe he just wanted to be less serious.

We lived in a small town, and there were lots of places to explore: woods, creeks, and fields. I desperately wanted to stumble upon a mystery and was always on the lookout for clues. But to no avail. Nothing, I decided, ever happened in Grover's Fork, and nothing ever would.

After fourth grade and the Hardy Boys, I would never again be content with my small-town life. Eventually, we moved away to Atlanta, and I discovered that you also could be isolated among a crowd. But that's another story.

Writers have been inspiring wonder and wanderlust at least since Homer put pen to parchment back in the 8th Century B.C. I happened to discover the Hardy Boys first, and they sparked in me a love of reading that eventually would lead to Homer and a taste for adventure that would take me on my own odyssey.

Joel Stewart, former City Editor at the *Birmingham Star-Ledger*, is a contributing editor for *Alabama Magazine* and the author of *Crimson Voices: An Oral History of Alabama Football*. He grew up in Grover's Fork, Alabama, surrounded by cotton fields.

CHAPTER 10
THE SCHOOLHOUSE DOOR, PART I

"Color Barrier Falls Briefly at the University of Alabama," by Janet Bell, *New South Magazine,* May 1956, pp. 7-9.

A cold rain fell on the University of Alabama campus on Feb. 3, 1956. For Autherine Lucy, whose four-year odyssey to become the first Negro student in the University's 135-year history was finally ending, a little rain was the least of her concerns.

Lucy, the youngest of nine children of a Marengo County farmer, first applied to the university in 1952 following graduation from Birmingham's Miles College. Polly Myers, a fellow Miles College graduate, applied at the same time. They received dormitory assignments and letters of welcome from University President Dr. John M. Gallalee.

But when they tried to register in September 1952, Dean of Admissions William F. Adams informed them that a mistake had been made: Alabama law prohibited their admittance.

Enter Arthur Shores, a Birmingham attorney who was representing the two women. After his formal appeal to Dr. Gallalee to admit the women were ignored, Shores filed suit in U.S. District Court in Birmingham. The suit, filed on behalf of all qualified Negro students, asked for an injunction prohibiting the university from denying them admission.

Attorneys for the university argued that the suit was unconstitutional, and District Court Judge H. Hobart Grooms agreed. President Dwight D. Eisenhower had appointed Grooms, a native of Kentucky, to the federal bench in 1953. Shores appealed the ruling to the Fifth Circuit Court of Appeals in New Orleans, which refused to overturn the original ruling.

As the case wound its way through the federal judiciary, Lucy took a teaching job in Carthage, Miss. Myers married, became a mother, and filed for divorce. Later, the university would cite this series of events as justification for their rejection of Myers' application.

On May 17, 1954, the U.S. Supreme Court announced its decision outlawing segregation in public education. In light of the *Brown vs. Board of Education of Topeka, Kansas* decision, attorneys for Lucy and Myers amended their suit and returned to Judge Grooms' court.

On June 29, 1955, Judge Grooms delivered his historic decision: The university could not deny Lucy and Myers admission because of their race. Subsequently, he ruled that the decision was a class action, and no qualified Negro could be denied admission.

Grooms granted the university a four-month delay in implementing the decision while it appealed. When in late December 1955, the Fifth Circuit Court upheld Judge Grooms' ruling, the final legal obstacle was overcome.

On Jan. 31, 1956, Lucy received by registered mail a letter of acceptance from the university. Myers was denied admission because of her "conduct and marital record." Calling the rejection a "smear," she pledged to continue her efforts to enroll but gave up shortly thereafter.

On the night of Jan. 31, four crosses were burned on the university campus. More crosses were burned on Feb. 1, the day that Lucy registered.

A few minutes before 9:00 a.m. on a wet Feb. 3, Lucy arrived at Smith Hall for her first class, Geography I. Wearing a raincoat and hat over a light orange blouse and skirt, she slipped into the classroom and took a seat in the front row. Avoided by the other students, she sat alone.

The class over, she walked across campus to her next class at Graves Hall, followed closely by a policeman. Out of the rain, under eaves, and in doorways, curious students watched her progress. Later, her classes over for the day, a relieved Lucy returned to her room. The first day had passed without trouble. Lucy now had the weekend to regroup and prepare for Monday.

That night, however, more crosses were burned on campus, attracting a crowd of 1200 students who exploded fireworks and sang "Dixie." The following night, an even larger crowd gathered, and non-students were observed among the crowd. The demonstration started out routinely enough with the crowd marching through the central campus chanting anti-Lucy epithets. But ominously, the crowd morphed into a mob, which attacked passing cars and a bus. The following day, Sunday, was quiet, likely because of a light rain that fell throughout the day.

On Monday morning, a crowd began forming early near Smith Hall. When Lucy arrived for her 9:00 a.m. class, the crowd numbered about 150. Tuscaloosa Police Chief W.C. Tompkins noted that non-students, primarily rubber workers from the Goodyear plant in town, made up a majority of the crowd. The crowd was in an ugly mood and shouts of "kill her" had officials worried.

Exiting Smith Hall, Lucy was spirited into the Dean of Women Sarah Healey's car. The crowd spotted the escape attempt and hurled rocks at the departing car. By 11:00 a.m. when Lucy's second class ended, the crowd had swelled to 2,000.

About 11:40 a.m., a Negro surrounded by three police officers appeared at the front entrance of Graves Hall. With the crowd's attention diverted, the police escorted Lucy out a back entrance and into a waiting highway patrol car. Lucy didn't know it, but she wouldn't be back.

As the drama on campus was unfolding, the University Board of Trustees was meeting. Their decision, announced later in the day, barred Lucy from campus "for the public safety." Reaction was swift. Arthur Shores demanded immediate reinstatement. Dr. Oliver C. Carmichael, who had succeeded Dr. Gallalee as the university president, asked Gov. James Folsom for National Guard assistance. Folsom denied the request while claiming that he was "ready at all times to meet with any situation properly."

His demand for reinstatement unheeded, Shores petitioned the courts. At this point, Lucy's attorneys made a regrettable misstep. In her suit for readmittance, Lucy charged university officials with conspiring with the mob—a gratuitous and impossible-to-prove charge. Judge Grooms allowed Lucy to delete the charge from her suit, but the damage had been done.

On Feb. 29, Grooms ordered the university to reinstate Lucy. Fast on the heels of the decision, the Board of Trustees met and expelled Lucy, citing her charges of conspiracy as the reason. Although she promised to continue her struggle to attend the university, Lucy soon married a Texas minister, the Rev. Hugh Foster, and moved to Texas.

Although it ended badly, Lucy's attempt to integrate the University of Alabama did establish legal precedent for later efforts. Judge Grooms' ruling that no qualified Negro can be denied admittance to the university on the basis of their race remains the law of the land. The clock is ticking.

Janet Bell is a reporter for the *Montgomery Observer*.

****

May 5, 1956

Dear Mildred,

I just wanted to send you a copy of my article for the *New South Magazine* on the Lucy affair. There was so much that we didn't have space for in the paper that I wanted to add to the coverage. Plus, a magazine piece gave me the freedom to be more humanistic in telling the story.

I must admit that I was surprised that the paper allowed me to cover the story. I'd been working overtime covering the boycott story, and it had flared up again with the firebombing at Rev. King's home just days before Autherine arrived on campus, but Mac let me go anyway. We had to cover it. It was almost as big a story as the boycott.

Of course, the university prevailed in the end. I had hoped that Autherine would stay and fight, but that was her decision. Her ordeal would have scared the bejesus out of me. It is somewhat encouraging that the university expelled her for slandering it. They didn't argue that she had no legal right to attend.

They know that the law has turned decidedly against them, and they're trying to find a way to kick this can down the road. That's what passes for leadership in Alabama these days. Even Folsom stuck his head in the sand. President Carmichael pleaded for the governor to send National Guard troops to restore order, but Folsom refused. He did say that he was watching the situation and would respond "properly." Whatever that means. It could have been worse though. He could have cheered on the mob.

The *Brown* decision, the bus boycott, and the Lucy affair have really muddied the political waters here. Membership in the local White Citizens' Council has doubled during the boycott. That's a bad sign. Lots of these people are relatively harmless on their own, but in a crowd, they become braver. The average politician, of course, doesn't want to get on the wrong side of things.

So, even a racial moderate like Folsom is hedging his bets. Politics, it seems, attracts very few angels.

I've decided that once the boycott ends—and it has to end eventually, right?—that I'm going to take a leave of absence and write a book about it. I've covered it from the beginning, and I have tons of interview material that I haven't used. Now that the national press has discovered the story, there should be an audience for a book. We'll see.

I've already contacted a publisher who's expressed interest. I worked up a couple of sample chapters covering the background and the early days of the boycott, and if they like it, I believe they'll green light the project. Keep your fingers crossed.

Enough about me. Has James' Little League season officially started? I know he's excited. I hope that he's not expecting too much too soon. He's only ten and playing with kids as much as two years older. That's a big difference at that age. I'm happy that he and Joel ended up on the same team. Take a Polaroid of him in his uniform for me. Send me a list of their games, and I'll try to time my next visit so that I can see him play. Is he a centerfielder like Mickey Mantle? He told me last Christmas that he hoped to get the number 7. I bet that's a popular one, and the older boys likely get first crack.

Another month and you're free for the summer. Other than lots of baseball games, how do you plan to keep busy? Now that James is older, you must have lots of extra free time when he's at baseball practice, the swimming pool, or off to the picture show with Joel.

Please don't start watching those daytime serials that are all the rage. I've seen snatches of them, and I can promise you that nobody will mistake them for Shakespeare. Although, I imagine that they borrow heavily from the Bard's tropes: love, lust, ambition, revenge, deception, et.al. The fundamental ingredients for drama haven't changed since Shakespeare. Since Homer actually. Of course, based on what I've seen, there aren't any Shakespeare's writing for television.

It is interesting though that Shakespeare and Homer wrote for a popular audience. So, perhaps television will eventually attract a few genuine talents. Hollywood certainly did.

Hope to see you sooner than later.

Love,
Janet

****

September 10, 1956

Dear Janet,

Wow! Congratulations on the book contract. You're going to be famous. Most likely to succeed, indeed. I hope you remember your old friends when you're rich and famous, at least your oldest and best friend.

I'm sure that you watched *The Ed Sullivan Show* last night. How could you not have? Elvis' appearance is all that anyone talked about last week. I've never seen James so excited about anyone not named Mickey Mantle. He's certainly not Sinatra, but young people today don't want their parents' music. I understand that, but did it have to be rock and roll?

For us "older" listeners, I think Elvis is a shock because he's so openly sexual. His voice isn't necessarily bad, but I'm not buying his records, yet anyway. I guess that he's attractive in a James Dean sort of way. I did like the ballad he sang last night, "Love Me Tender." I'm not a fan of things like "Hound Dog" though. What does that mean anyway?

Elvis' movie is coming out in November. Joel's dad said that he expects to get prints in December. He usually runs a minor film during the week and a more popular film over the weekend, but he hopes to run the Elvis movie all week. I promised James that we'd go. The theater will probably be packed for every showing. I hope that the teenage girls don't scream like they did on television last night. Tell me that I'm not getting old.

James is settling into fifth grade. He's in Mrs. Green's class. Yes, she's still around. She seemed like an old-timer when we had her. That was what, almost twenty-five years ago? But she hasn't changed much. James likes her so there's that. I like her because she finds ways to keep kids interested.

Yes, she hands out the dreaded word lists that have to be memorized and gives regular quizzes on the lists, but every couple of weeks, she has a classroom spelling bee that includes all the lists from the first week of school. It's a fun way to check their progress. I think that James, being as competitive as he is, will enjoy those spelling bees.

I had a visit from Mike Thomas just before school started. He wanted to let me know that there's nothing to report on Roger. It seems that everybody has moved on: the FBI, State Police, and even the county sheriff. It's officially what they call a "Cold Case."

It's hard to believe that someone can disappear without a trace, but that's what Roger seems to have done. I continue to believe that he's alive somewhere. But seriously, I've moved on. I think that, for the most part, James has too. He acted up some in the beginning, but that seems to have stopped. I still worry though. How could something like this not leave scars?

As much as I dislike Ernest, we still go over for Sunday dinner. James is their grandchild, and I feel so sorry for Mrs. Morgan. Ernest only loves himself of course, but he tries to win James over by spoiling him. If James mentions something he wants—a new bike most recently—it doesn't matter that I tell Ernest no. A few days later, there's a new bike on the front porch.

I don't like it, but considering what James has gone through, I can't very well make him give it back. But I know there's a price to pay. With Ernest, there's always a price to pay. At least, I'm not blind to what's going on. Forewarned is forearmed, right?

I need to put supper together before James starves.

Love,
Mildred

****

December 12, 1956

Dear Mildred,

Just a short note since I'll be seeing you soon. I'll be home only a couple of days. I plan to drive down on Christmas Eve and return to Montgomery on the day after Christmas. The paper approved my request for six months of leave to get the book done, so I can't waste any time. The publisher wants to rush it into publication while the story is still fresh. They are talking about a late fall (1957!) publication date. I've done most of the research and some of the writing already, but I'll probably write 10 hours a day, seven days a week until it's finished.

The boycott will officially end on the 20th when a new Montgomery ordinance allowing integrated seating goes into effect. That works out to 381 days since the boycott began. So, I'm thinking of calling the book *381 Days: The Montgomery Bus Boycott*. What do you think? I suggested it to my editor, and he likes it, so we'll see. I really don't care what they call it, I just want to get it done.

I bought James a couple of Hardy Boys books and Elvis' single of "Blue Suede Shoes" for Christmas. The B-side is "Tutti Frutti." Think of it as a present for both of you. Ha!

Don't despair. I've got something special for you.

See you soon,
Janet

****

"Love Me Tender," by Joel Stewart, *Alabama Magazine*, December 2008, pp. 4-5.

My kids never understood my fascination with Elvis. Of course, they didn't know the original Elvis, or even the brief reincarnation of the original Elvis in the late 1960s. What little they knew was mostly from the grotesque and tragic Third Act when Elvis was a bloated shadow of his old self. More like a parody.

But they humored me when I insisted that they call Elvis the King of Rock and Roll. Occasionally, one of them would suggest another title—the Burger King was a favorite—but I took it in stride. I was just happy that they didn't point out that he died on the throne.

I was among the first wave of the Baby Boom generation, and we grew up with Elvis. Indeed, he was the first public figure to truly fire our collective imagination. Our parents liked Ike and Sinatra. That was reason enough for us to look elsewhere for icons. And if our parents found Elvis a little dangerous, all the better.

Dangerous certainly described the young Elvis. He sang rock and roll music and moved his hips provocatively, and our parents reacted like he was Attila the Hun. When a reluctant Ed Sullivan first booked Elvis for his Sunday night variety show on CBS, he insisted that the cameras avoid the gyrating pelvis. So, we Boomers quite naturally embraced Elvis and anointed him King. British rockers would eventually invade and knock the King off his throne, but by then, Elvis had become embedded in our memories of growing up.

I watched Elvis on *Ed Sullivan* in 1956, and I saw his movie debut in *Love Me Tender* later that year. My dad operated the local picture show, and I got to see the movie twice. Elvis played a Texas farmer during the Civil War. It was a dramatic role, and he sang only a handful of tunes, including the title song. The critics praised his performance, but it was the last serious role Elvis played in a movie career that traded shamelessly on his star power.

As I grew older, I started working part-time at the picture show, and I saw a lot more of Elvis. The titles of those films say it all: *Jailhouse Rock*, *Viva Las Vegas*, *Fun In Acapulco*. Pretty girls, exotic scenery, and rock and roll. The critics hated it, but fans loved it. My dad always smiled when he got a new Elvis movie because he knew that the shows would be packed.

Elvis even went along on my first date. I was sixteen and a sophomore. I double-dated with my best friend, James, who had gotten a Volkswagen Beetle for his sixteenth birthday. Instead of the picture show in town, we drove twelve miles to a drive-in. My date was also a sophomore, but this was definitely not her first date. In that alone, we made a very odd couple.

Her name was Fran, which was short for Frances. Even now, over forty years later, I can't fathom what possessed me to ask her out, or an even greater mystery, what possessed her to accept.

The movie that evening was *Blue Hawaii* and starred Elvis in paradise. Elvis sang some songs, made all the right moves, and got the girl. Me, I survived the evening somehow. I never asked Fran out again. I'm not sure that she even noticed. But you never forget your first date, and Fran—and Elvis—are forever hardwired into my memory.

Soon after that first date, surfer music arrived from California to challenge His Majesty. Then, The Beatles invaded. Elvis continued to churn out insipid movies and soundtracks, but he was increasingly irrelevant to the Boomers. He briefly revived his career in the late sixties, but following his separation from his wife, Priscilla, in 1972, he spiraled out of control. Finally, overweight and dependent on prescription drugs, he died of heart failure at his Memphis estate on August 16, 1977. The King was dead.

I was in my car on I-65 in Birmingham when I heard the news. I had the radio on loud because the disk jockey was playing one of my favorite songs, "The Weight," by perhaps the best group ever, The Band. When the disk jockey abruptly broke in, I uttered a curse. What could be important enough to interrupt "The Weight"? A nuclear attack? Okay, sure. A stock market crash? Well, maybe. Elvis' death? Absolutely.

For the next hour, the station played Elvis songs nonstop without commercials. They never did get back to "The Weight." I remembered that the flip side of "The Weight" was "I Shall Be Released." How appropriate is that?

Song after song triggered a memory of growing up. That, I decided, multiplied by a generation, was quite a legacy. Long live the King.

Joel Stewart, former City Editor at the *Birmingham Star-Ledger*, is a contributing editor for *Alabama Magazine* and the author of *Crimson Voices: An Oral History of Alabama Football*. He grew up in Grover's Fork, Alabama, surrounded by cotton fields.

CHAPTER 11
SCHOOL DAYS II

January 28, 1957

Dear Janet,

Oh my God. If I hear "Tutti Frutti" one more time, I can't be held responsible for what I do. Has there ever been anything so inane? You did this to punish me for something, but I can't imagine what would deserve this. James, on the other hand, can't get enough of it. He even sings along. What has happened to my normal little boy?

I have to listen to "Hound Dog" several times a day. I'm not sure if the lyrics are appropriate for an eleven-year-old. To be fair, I bought him "Love Me Tender" and a used guitar for his birthday. More on that later.

Ballads, I don't mind. Rock and roll takes a little—or a lot—getting used to. Something good might come out of it, though. James was never really interested in music before. Now, he wants to learn to play guitar. I talked with Mr. Morton, the band director at school, and he recommended Neal Daley of all people. You remember Neal, the rural mail carrier. It seems that he plays in a country music band on the weekends. Well, Neal agreed to teach James and even sold us one of his old guitars. He explained to me that he liked to start kids out with used guitars in case they didn't stick with it. James began lessons two weeks ago. So far, so good.

Speaking of presents, I finally got around to reading *Peyton Place,* and no, I won't be passing it on to my mother. Whatever I do with it, I have to get it out of the house before James stumbles upon it. Peyton Place is definitely not the sort of place where the Hardy Boys would live. Nothing salacious ever happens in Bayport. Villainous? Yes. Salacious? Never. On the other hand, how honest do we really want our children's books to be? That was me speaking as a mother, not a school librarian.

I can see why *Peyton Place* is so popular. It's got everything: lust, illicit sex, and murder, not to mention small-town hypocrisy. Maybe you should write a similar novel and replace the fictional Peyton Place with a fictional Grover's Fork. I'd be careful if I were you, though. Lots of people around here read the *Observer*, and you aren't as popular as you were when you covered society. I wonder how popular Grace Metalious is in her hometown these days.

I've been thinking about Roger this past week. Coach Jackson is leaving Grover's Fork after spring semester. He's going to coach at a big high school in Columbus. I tried to tell Roger that Frank would either win and leave for a better job or lose and be fired. Roger was convinced that he'd win and stay to become principal and maybe superintendent.

That was a big part of Roger's melancholy—or was it depression? But only a part. The biggest part was the long shadow of Ernest over his life. It was that shadow that he had to escape. Maybe I should have majored in psychology instead of library science.

Roger's been gone three years this month. It seems like longer. Wherever he is, I hope he's found some peace.

How's work on the book going?

Love,
Mildred

****

"Observer Reporters Win Pulitzer," by Bill Thomas. *The Montgomery Observer*, April 18, 1957, p 1.

Observer reporters, Janet Bell and Earl Thomas, have been awarded the Pulitzer Prize for Local Reporting for their yearlong coverage of the Montgomery bus boycott. The Pulitzer Prize honors achievements in journalism and literature and was funded by legendary publisher, Joseph Pulitzer.

Columbia University administers the Prizes, which have been awarded annually since 1917 in several categories. The Pulitzer Prize Board selects the winners in each category from nominated entries. The Prize comes with a $10,000 award.

The Prize Board Jury for Local Reporting cited Bell and Thomas for their in-depth and clear-headed coverage of a seismic event in the struggle for civil rights among Negroes. They also praised their effort to report on all sides in the conflict and their dedication to a story that played out over many months.

Observer publisher, Glenn Smith, noted that the Pulitzer was the most prestigious honor in American journalism and lauded the reporting of Bell and Thomas and the behind-the-scenes direction of City Editor Robert MacArthur.

"It's not often that you get a local story with national interest and implications," Smith said, "and when you do, it's important that you have the editors and reporters to do it justice. That's what makes this award so special: It's an endorsement of the kind of work that we do around here every day."

See "Pulitzer," p. 4

****

"Tense Times in Little Rock," by Jerrold Cooper, *The Wiregrass Herald*, September 25, 1957, p. 1.

(SPA) Little Rock, Arkansas: The Little Rock Nine returned to Central High School today under the watchful eyes of the Army's famed 101st Airborne Division. The nine Negro students first integrated the school on September 23 but were removed in the face of escalating violence.

When Arkansas Gov. Orval Faubus refused to act to protect the Negro students, President Dwight D. Eisenhower signed an order deploying the 327th Airborne Battle Group to Little Rock and nationalized the entire Arkansas National Guard.

Eisenhower's swift action sent a clear signal to Faubus that the president would use the power of his office to enforce the Supreme Court's *Board vs. Board of Education* decision outlawing segregated schools. With some southern governors pledging "massive resistance" to the enforcement of the *Brown* decision and Faubus openly questioning the authority of the federal courts, Eisenhower's order was welcomed by some and reviled by others.

Angry crowds gathered near the school as airborne soldiers escorted the nine Negro students in, but they did nothing to interfere with the soldiers.

See "Little Rock," p. 7

****

September 30, 1957

Dear Mildred,

I'm sure that you're watching the news about Little Rock. It looks like this effort might succeed because of Ike's intervention. Autherine Lucy might still be a student at the university if Big Jim had taken a forceful stand. But he didn't, so we'll have to replay that drama.

It pains me that people just can't accept that the schools are going to be integrated. And not just the schools. Society too. You can't fight the Supreme Court. It's just a matter of how and when it happens. Why can't we just accept it and move on? It drives me crazy. I know—we all know—otherwise rational people who simply refuse to think logically about race. Sometimes I wonder if we'll ever move beyond this divide.

My book is in production as I write. The goal is to have it in the bookstores by Thanksgiving. The people at the publisher think that the Little Rock showdown will help the book. I hate to think like that, but they have to sell books to stay in business. They also were overjoyed with the Pulitzer and intend to use that heavily in promoting the book. I can't argue with their strategy. I want people to read it too. As many as possible. Even in Grover's Fork.

I rode the city buses last week for a post-boycott story, and it depressed me. Despite the new ordinance allowing Negroes to sit just about anywhere they choose, many have gone back to self-segregating. I'm sure that the violence after the desegregation order went into effect likely cowed many riders, especially the older ones. Who wants to be shot or beaten up just so they can ride in the front of the bus? Who am I to ask people to take risks that I probably wouldn't take? I hate being a hypocrite. So, in a way, we're just about back where we started.

One thing that came out of the boycott that I think is permanent is Rev. King's leadership role in the civil rights movement. He's smart, charismatic, and articulate. Just what you need for the face of a movement. His embrace of civil disobedience is a brilliant stroke in what is essentially a battle for hearts and minds. Reminds me of the Chinese military strategist Sun Tzu's advice to military commanders: Seize the high ground. He was talking about geography, of course, but in this struggle, it's going to be the moral high ground that counts most.

I'm glad to hear that James is liking sixth grade. It's a pivotal year. The last chance to really be a kid. Everything changes in junior high. I don't think that I've ever been as unhappy as junior high. I remember hanging on to you for ballast. How do kids survive junior high without a safe harbor of some sort? You were mine. Thank you. Better late than never.

Does James like Buddy Holly? The DJ on "Housewives Hit Parade" on WBAM plays his records sometimes. It's rock and roll, but not as raucous as Elvis. The soft side of rock and roll. His latest single, "That'll Be the Day," is popular right now, and he's just released a new one, "Peggy Sue," that's really catchy. I'm sure that you'll like them more than "Hound Dog."

Bye,
Janet

****

New South Magazine, December 1957

Featured Review by David Harden

381 Days: The Story of the Montgomery Bus Boycott, by Janet Bell, New York: Contemporary Books, 1957, 364pp.

Janet Bell, who shared a Pulitzer Prize with her colleague, Earl Thomas, for their reporting on the Montgomery Bus Boycott, reprises the saga in greater detail in this first-rate account. Bell, a native Alabaman and a veteran political reporter at *The Montgomery Observer*, writes with a light hand, allowing the protagonists to fill in their portrait with their own words. When it works, and it works more often than not, it can be devastating.

The boycott began on Dec. 5, 1955, after a local seamstress, Rosa Parks, was arrested for refusing to give up her seat to a white man and continued for the 381 days in the title until Dec. 20, 1956. During that time, Montgomery's Negro community walked, biked, and carpooled to work.

The boycott was the inspiration of long-time local civil rights advocate, E.D. Nixon, but the face of the effort was an obscure young minister, the Rev. Martin Luther King, Jr. Articulate and apparently intrepid, King stood fast throughout the long ordeal and emerged as a national figure in the civil rights movement. Even when his home was firebombed, King counseled non-violence. Look for that tactic to guide the movement in the future.

The drama ebbs and flows as it surely did during the long days of the boycott, but Bell keeps the narrative simmering with vivid details of the everyday challenges faced by the participants. One of her greatest strengths is her familiarity with the local Negro community—a familiarity that clearly predated the boycott. It allows her to eavesdrop as King and his lieutenants plan their moves, and it gives her account a sense of balance that eluded many reporters.

Bell seems clear that King and the thousands of ordinary citizens who took a stand (walk?) against discrimination are the heroes of the boycott, but she isn't as direct about naming the villains. She doesn't excuse the white mobs that appear like mushrooms after a rain when the issue of racial justice is raised or the whites that favor racial change but are cowed into silence by the mobs. But she saves her vitriol for the political, economic, and community leaders who disappear when their leadership is most needed. Or worse, when they exploit the situation for personal gain.

In the end, the U.S. Supreme Court ruled against the Montgomery Bus Co., and the Montgomery City Council passed an ordinance desegregating the city's buses. But that's only one battle in what promises to be a long struggle to topple Jim Crow. This fall, the skirmish moved to Little Rock, Ark. Who knows where it goes tomorrow. But if you want an inside look at the contours of the battleground, *381 Days* is a good place to start.

David Harden is Assistant Professor of History at North Alabama College and the author of *Reconstruction in the Alabama Black Belt*.

****

December 8, 1957

Dear Janet,

Thanks for sending the book, autographed no less. I decided to keep it pristine, so I bought another copy to read. What can I say? It's great. You are even more talented than I thought. Since I had followed your stories in the paper, it wasn't as dramatic as it will be for someone who didn't have access to your original reporting. I've seen a few reviews, all good. I bet it's going to be a hit.

Lots of people around school and town are talking about the book, mostly those who approve of it, at least in my presence. I'm sure that there are those who think that you've gone over to the other side, but they don't share their thoughts with me.

There's no way that they can ignore you, though: First, a Pulitzer and now this book, but if I were you, I wouldn't hold my breath until they put up a statue of you in the park. If anybody gets a statue, it'll probably be Ernest. Maybe in time—probably a long time, I'm afraid—they'll erect a billboard out on the highway coming into town: "Welcome to Grover's Fork: Hometown of Janet Bell."

I can't believe how quickly Christmas is coming up. If you listen to the Alabama fans around town, it's already come. Santa, of course, brought Coach Bryant back to Alabama. I don't think that the Bama graduates at school have stopped smiling since the announcement last week.

Auburn fans claim not to be concerned, but they are; or they should be. Bama fans have gone through quite a drought lately, but they seem convinced that they've finally got their rainmaker. I don't know much about football, but Bryant has won everywhere he's been, even Kentucky. And he looks like a football coach. I wouldn't bet against him.

Maybe I should order James an Alabama sweatshirt for Christmas. I have a feeling Santa might be leaving more of them under Alabama trees this Christmas Eve. The fact is that I don't have much of a list; worse, I don't have many ideas.

James seems interested in two things: baseball and music. His baseball mitt is hardly broken in good, so that's not an option. I'm sure that I'll buy him some records, rock and roll, of course. He's already given me a list. I'll choose a few and send you a list of what's left. He still enjoys the *Hardy Boys*, so there's that. He now has the first eight titles in the series. I'm hoping to find nine and ten, but I'll defer to you if you want.

James was slower to take to Buddy Holly than he was to Elvis, but he's on board now. He bought "Peggy Sue," and he's learning to play it on his guitar. James actually has a decent singing voice and sounds fine singing Buddy Holly stuff. Elvis is more of a stretch for him; not ballads like "Love Me Tender," but the frenetic stuff like "Hound Dog." That would be a stretch for lots of people, including Frank Sinatra.

I've been wondering when someone like Sinatra was going to sound off about rock and roll. Well, it finally happened in an interview last month. I don't know if you saw it, but it was harsh.

No, harsh is an understatement. More like brutal. So much so that I didn't share it with James. Among other things, he called it a "rancid-smelling aphrodisiac." It may be, but I just didn't want to have to explain what an aphrodisiac is to James. You can't read the interview without concluding that Sinatra is worried that rock and roll has already won.

I misspoke earlier when I said that James is only interested in baseball and music. Since the Soviets launched their Sputnik satellite in October, he's become curious about space. We even went outside a few nights to try to spot Sputnik as it passed over.

Sputnik surprised everybody that I know; maybe shocked is a more accurate term. How could the backward Soviets be first in space? Surely, they stole the technology from us, but maybe not if this week's failed launch of an American satellite is any indication. The worst thing is that the launch was televised, so all the world could see our rocket exploding on the launch pad; not a good look. I expect that Eisenhower will have some explaining to do.

We don't have much on space exploration in the school library, but we do have a series of young adult novels about space by Robert Heinlein, the science fiction writer. James has read a couple of them and is intrigued, so I might see if I can't get him something from the series.

I'm not a fan of science fiction—call me a literary snob— but Heinlein is one of the masters of the genre. I've also thought about ordering Isaac Asimov's *The Martian Way* for him. It's written for an adult audience, but James reads at an advanced level. Anyway, he needs to be challenged occasionally. And no, I'm not biased. I can show you his scores from the California Achievement Test if you're interested.

Once I figure out what to get James, I still have my parents and sis and you. What do you get someone who already has a Pulitzer Prize? See my problem?

I can hardly wait to see you at Christmas.

Bye,
Mildred

P.S. Most people don't know this, but Coach Bryant's wife, Mary Harmon, is a native of the Wiregrass from just down the road in Pike County. So, I guess that we should go ahead and jump on the bandwagon. Roll Tide!

****

"Walking on Water," by Joel Stewart, *Alabama Magazine*, September 2008, pp. 7-8.

In the Alabama of my youth, cotton was king, the schools were segregated, most folks were poor, and the churches were full on Sunday morning. National surveys of progress regularly ranked the state near the bottom in such things as per capita income and literacy. In the media and national culture, we were routinely portrayed as hicks and rednecks. The columnist and critic, H.L. Mencken, once dismissed the entire region as a cultural Sahara.

Others said much worse. Even as a youngster, I was ashamed and resentful and often wished that I lived elsewhere. California sounded cool. I wasn't alone. The state suffered from a collective inferiority complex. Not that we admitted it; that would be too painful, so we defended what we could, rationalized what we couldn't, and apologized for nothing. It was an unholy catechism that only sounded brave.

About the only thing where we ranked near the top was church attendance. Our license plates proclaimed Alabama as the

"Heart of Dixie," but the state also was at the center of the "Bible Belt"—a broad swath of rural America that embraced fundamental Christianity. Ironically, it was among these devout, born-again Christians that a new (secular) religion, complete with a patron saint, monumental temples, and a sacred shrine would emerge in the late 1950s.

The new religion was Alabama football, and its patron saint was Paul "Bear" Bryant, the head coach at the University of Alabama. Alabama football held its public services at Denny Stadium in Tuscaloosa on the university campus and at Legion Field in nearby Birmingham in front of large, enthusiastic crowds of worshippers. There were widespread reports of miracles, and posters and T-shirts depicted the Bear walking on water. After his retirement and untimely death, the devout erected a shrine to him in Tuscaloosa, and thousands of pilgrims visit annually.

I was still in grammar school when Coach Bryant arrived in Tuscaloosa in 1958 to revive a once-proud program that had fallen on hard times. Very hard times. Even then, at the beginning, he looked like a savior—tall, handsome, and charismatic. One of his former players, George Blanda, said that when he first saw Bryant, he thought, *This must be what God looks like.*

The new coach took the state by storm, turning the team around in a single season. In 1961, he won the first of six national championships at Alabama. We loved him. No, we worshipped him. Because of him, we were first in something. We might be forty-eighth in per-pupil spending and forty-seventh in family income, but we were number one in football. A legend was born.

I was a child of the fifties, baseball's golden age, and I was passionate about little else as a boy. I thought that football and basketball existed to keep us out of trouble while we waited for spring. High school football was popular, but I rarely heard anyone mention college football unless it was the week of the Alabama-Auburn game. And professional football was mostly a rumor in the South.

The Bear changed all that. People couldn't get enough. Before long, his Sunday afternoon highlight show was the most popular program on local television. We planned our day around it, and for an hour, much of the state shut down. We hung on his every word: listen to your mamas and papas; act like a winner; and never, ever arm tackle. We had heard all the stories. How, as a young man in Arkansas, he had wrestled a bear and won! How, as a football player at Alabama, he had suffered a broken leg and played on.

After the Bear's arrival, I never considered attending any college except Alabama, not even after we moved to Atlanta in 1963. I arrived in Tuscaloosa in September 1964 amid dramatic changes at the university and in the state. Segregation was beginning to crumble, and African American students had enrolled at the university in 1963.

I wish I could say that the state had succumbed to reason, justice, and compassion, but I'd be lying. We had yielded to the authority of the national government in a televised spectacle featuring the governor standing in the schoolhouse door, but progress is progress. There were no African Americans on the football team yet. Coach Bryant judged people by their character and would eventually recruit African Americans, but he moved cautiously. Much too cautiously for some, but when he finally moved, he never faltered.

The star of the 1964 team was a Yankee: Joe Willie Namath from Beaver Falls, Pennsylvania, but we loved him like a native son. Joe Willie led us to a national championship in 1964 and went on to even greater fame in the National Football League. He led the New York Jets to an improbable victory in the 1967 Super Bowl on his way to being enshrined at the Pro Football Hall of Fame. And if he looked good in shoulder pads and a helmet, he looked even better in mink coats and panty hose.

Coach Bryant won a third national championship in 1965, and the 1966 team led by the legendary Snake, Kenny Stabler, finished 11-0 but was denied a national championship by the polls.

Along the way, there were more than a few miracles, including one featuring the Snake in the rain at Legion Field against the hated Auburn Tigers.

I graduated from the university in 1968, but I continued to follow the Bear. He won three more national championships (1973, 1978, and 1979), and retired in 1982 with the record for most wins among college coaches. He died suddenly on January 26, 1983, of a heart attack. As the motorcade bearing his body made its way along I-59 from Tuscaloosa to Birmingham for burial, it passed a banner hanging from an overpass. The banner read, "God needed a coach." Amen.

I believe that we worshiped the Bear not only because he resurrected our football team but also because he revived a bit of our self-respect. Our political and civic leaders had failed us—clinging stubbornly to failed policies—and Coach Bryant, larger than life, filled the void. He took a bunch of mostly undersized and underestimated young men and taught them how to be winners. Along the way, he showed us all the way to the Promised Land.

Joel Stewart, former City Editor at the *Birmingham Star-Ledger*, is a contributing editor for *Alabama Magazine* and the author of *Crimson Voices: An Oral History of Alabama Football*. He grew up in Grover's Fork, Alabama, surrounded by cotton fields.

CHAPTER 12
THE FIGHTING JUDGE: ROUND I

March 1, 1958

Dear Mildred,

You'll never guess who offered me a job: *The Atlanta Constitution*. Obviously, the Pulitzer has made me a valuable commodity. I doubt that they even knew I existed over in Atlanta before that. I can't say that I'm not pleased with the recognition. *The Constitution* is one of the most influential papers in the South. And I'd be making more money. Of course, it costs more to live in Atlanta than Montgomery. I'm also not convinced that I'd be better positioned professionally there than here in Montgomery.

I'm still convinced that the most important stories of the next few years are more likely to run through Alabama than Atlanta. Plus, Mac gives me a lot of freedom here—something I'd likely have to earn all over again at another paper. Believe me, I'm not afraid of the challenge. You know that. But I think the future here will be at least as challenging. So, I'm staying at the *Observer*. For now anyway. I hope I'm not making a mistake.

Anyway, how could I walk away from this year's governor's race? On the face of it, the choice facing Democratic voters is fairly stark. Attorney General Patterson is running as a dyed-in-the-wool segregationist. He has even publicly accepted the endorsement of the Ku Klux Klan, and he's already promised to close the schools before he'll integrate them. He's also campaigning as the law-and-order candidate, but more than anything, he's blatantly playing the race card. I guess we'll see how that works with the voters.

George Wallace is Patterson's most formidable rival. Years ago, Dick Hadley pointed him out at a political event of some kind and predicted that Wallace was going places. I didn't believe it at the time. I believe that I dismissed him as a little man with big ideas at the time. I guess I was wrong.

He was a state legislator at the time, but he barely made a ripple in the House. But since becoming a Circuit Judge, he's made quite a name for himself. "The fighting judge," the press calls him. Fighting for what is yet to be seen. He has a reputation as a moderate on race like his protégé Big Jim, and the NAACP has endorsed him.

I've only heard him speak once, and he focused on good roads and good schools, not race. I don't know what I expected, but he surprised me. He's more charismatic than he looks. In fact, he doesn't look charismatic at all. Until he opens his mouth. It should be an interesting and entertaining race. We also should learn something about where the state is headed in the next few years.

Spring break is almost upon us. Why don't you and James visit for a few days during the break? That's another reason to turn down the *Constitution*: Atlanta is much farther away from the people I love.

Tell James hello. I'm guessing that Little League will be gearing up soon. I hope to get down to see him play this summer. Who knows how long it'll be before even baseball is sacrificed on the altar of rock and roll? Ha.

Love,
Janet

****

"Patterson Tops Wallace in Primary Runoff," by Alex Smith, *The Wiregrass Herald*, June 25, 1958, p. 1.

Attorney General John Patterson handily defeated Third Circuit Court Judge George Wallace in the Democratic primary run-off yesterday. Following a close contest between the two in the June 3 primary, Patterson pulled away in the head-to-head matchup to win decisively. Patterson will now face William Longshore, the Republican nominee, in the November general election. Patterson will be a prohibitive favorite.

Patterson campaigned on his record of fighting crime as Attorney General and his outspoken support for segregation. Wallace, a racial moderate and protégé of Governor James Folsom, focused his campaign on economic development and increased funding for roads and schools.

Wallace openly refused to cooperate with the Ku Klux Klan, which endorsed Patterson. The NAACP backed Wallace, citing his record on the Third Circuit Court and his service as a member of the Board of Trustees of Tuskegee Institute.

Patterson, who will become the second youngest governor in Alabama history, thanked his supporters at a rally in Montgomery and promised to continue his efforts to rid Alabama of organized crime.

A subdued Wallace congratulated his opponent and pledged to keep fighting for the people of Alabama. Robert Fuller, a Wallace backer from Barbour County, noted that this was Wallace's first run for statewide office. "It's not the result we wanted," Fuller said, "but it's a solid start. The Judge will learn from this, and he'll be back in four years." Alluding to Wallace's success as a teenage boxer and his political sobriquet, "The Fighting Judge," Fuller warned, "This is a setback, but it's not a knockout. We'll be back."

See "Runoff," on p. 7

****

June 26, 1958

Dear Janet,

The talk of the town here isn't about Patterson but about Ernest. Nobody really expected Will Tucker to beat Ernest. Heck, nobody expected anybody to run against Ernest. He's run the county commission for so long that he's all that most voters know. Kind of like we felt about Roosevelt after a while.

Ernest tried to act like having a serious challenger was no big deal, but if he's smart, he'll take it seriously. He's treated the county like a personal fiefdom for too long, and some people are beginning to push back. The county is changing despite Ernest's agenda. Centerville is the only town in the county that's growing, and the civic leaders there are increasingly frustrated with the county commission. They almost lost out on the new Hill-Burton hospital because of the commission's tepid support. Plus, the commission flatly refused to help with the costs of improving access to the new mall going up on the north side of town.

Ernest relies on a ready supply of cheap, docile labor. Anything that offers workers a choice is a threat to his business model. At least that's the way he sees it. Lots of people around here see what's happening with the rural economy and are afraid. The local merchants look at the mall going in and wonder how many of their customers are going to drive an extra ten miles for more choices and lower prices. It won't take too many to leave to completely erode their profit margins.

Those people's livelihoods and social status are at stake. The Western Auto on Main Street closed last year. I know that others are struggling. The farmers and small-town merchants don't want change, and they see Ernest as their savior. So far, there are enough of them to keep Ernest on his throne, but history is not on their side. If trends continue, Centerville's population soon will be greater than the rest of the county combined. Anybody can do the math.

James and Joel have been working for Ernest this summer. I'd rather James didn't, but he wants to work. How can I discourage that? I feel better about it because Joel is there. Ernest will have to be on his best behavior, which isn't much, but it's something. Ernest is overpaying them, of course. He's trying to curry favor with James, but we'll see if that works. So far, James is enjoying the work. They were loading watermelons last week. It's hard work, but he's young. We'll see how he feels in August when cotton picking starts.

The boys made the All-Star Team. James made it last year, but Joel didn't. It's good to see Joel make it. When he's not pitching, James plays centerfield. The coaches wanted him to move to the infield, but he insists on centerfield like Mickey Mantle. Joel is playing first base. The season ends in a couple of weeks, and the All-Star District Tournament starts a week later. They play in Troy this year, but everybody says that we have a decent chance to win this year. Finally. It would be nice for the small-town boys to upset the city boys.

Any plans for the Fourth? I guess that we're going to spend it at the farm. Ernest invited James and Joel to come down and go fishing. I'm not crazy about baiting a hook, but it'll be fun for James. I worry that without a father, James is missing a lot. I try to do what

I can. You and I were never actually tomboys, though, so I'm learning on the job. If I do manage to catch something, I hope I don't fall in trying to land it.

Missing you,
Mildred

****

November 11, 1958

Dear Mildred,

Well, to nobody's surprise, John Patterson is our new governor. I'm not sure what to expect from a Patterson administration. He's against crime, but isn't everybody except the criminals? He's against racial integration, but name an Alabama politician who isn't. He says he's for better roads and schools. Just once, I'd like to hear a politician endorse washed-out roads and failing schools.

I guess he's for better schools if they're segregated. Didn't the Supreme Court rule that segregated schools were "inherently" unequal? So, he's for better schools for white children and unequal schools for Negro children, right? I don't know how much longer I can cover politics. I'm quickly becoming a cynic. You see enough hypocrisy and that happens, I guess.

On that subject, I had lunch last week with Dick Hadley, and he related a couple of ripe rumors floating around the Capitol. One has to do with Patterson and his extracurricular affairs, if you get my drift. I personally don't care what he does in his private life. Big Jim wasn't exactly husband of the year either.

The other, and probably more serious rumor, is about Judge Wallace. Seems that he blames his loss on being too moderate on race. He supposedly told his aide, Seymore Trammel, that nobody will ever "outnigger" him again. So, it doesn't matter what you actually believe. Or what's right. It only matters what will get you elected. The word on the street is that he's planning to run again in 1962. See my point? Ambition, thy name is hypocrisy.

Actually, hypocrisy has many fathers. Ambition. Fear. Desire. Remember Rev. Nelson? Upright, uptight, "sex is the devil's tool" Rev. Nelson? How many times did he say that? So often that it became banal. By junior high, we had to bite our tongues to keep from snickering.

Then, of course, he was caught with his pants down, literally, with a young wife he was "counseling." I guess that the devil made him do it. The "counseling" didn't help since the woman's husband filed for divorce. And left town. So did Rev. Nelson. Amazingly, the wife—ex-wife—stayed. She even remarried a few years later. Talk about chutzpah. I wouldn't have had that kind of courage. Anyway, we learned about hypocrisy early.

Speaking of men acting badly: I finally got my copy of *Lolita* last week. I had to order it special from the bookstore. I must admit that I didn't know much about Nabokov before now. I guess, like lots of other philistines, I was attracted by the controversy surrounding the manuscript. The reviews have been mixed. The *New York Times* reviewer called it "pretentious" and "dull, dull, dull." It's been selling like hotcakes but not so much in Montgomery. Probably not at all in Centerville.

The book is a lot of things, but it's not dull. On the surface, it's about pedophilia. Beneath the surface, though, it's about obsession. And carelessness. The oddly named protagonist Humbert Humbert's obsession with the nubile Lolita and Lolita's carelessness with her budding sexuality. At least that's my take. But I'll let you decide for yourself. If you haven't gotten a copy, hold off for a few weeks. I'll bring you my copy at Thanksgiving. If you like it, maybe you'll buy a copy for the school library. Ha! There hasn't been a book burning in Grover's Fork. Yet.

I usually don't like stories of obsession. Ahab. Hamlet. Heathcliff. Maybe they strike too close to home. Poppa seldom offers me advice; that's what Mom's for, I guess, and she never hesitates. But he warned me a few years back that success is a demanding master. What can I say? I am ambitious, and I won't apologize for it. I just hope that my ambition isn't an obsession. But how will I know? You'll tell me before a whale swallows me, right?

Have you seen Rev. King's book on the boycott? I'm sure that it'll sell well. Just not here in Montgomery. At least that's been my experience. Maybe once you've lived something, you're not as anxious to relive it. The book's appearance probably will mean fewer future sales for me, but I knew that I'd have competition eventually.

While the books are competitors, they are different in important ways. Mine is journalistic; his is a first-person account told from a particular point of view. That's not a judgment in any way, it's just a fact. He knows things that only an insider could know: Important things that add another layer to the story.

If my book has an advantage, it's that I don't (can't) pick sides. Not that you could convince my many critics of that. And as you well know, I do have a side, but I try to keep that out of my reporting. It's not my job to tell people what to think, but to give them the facts and let them decide. Maybe one day I'll move over to the editorial side of the paper, and then, I'll happily share my views.

Mac asked me if I wanted to cover the book's local release, but I declined. I'm surprised that he even asked. I am obviously not an uninterested party. He gave the story to Earl, which really was the only appropriate choice. Earl did a nice story and even managed to work in a plug (well, at least a mention) for my book.

See you soon,
Janet

****

"Reliving the Bus Boycott from the Inside," by Earl Thomas, *The Montgomery Observer*, October 1, 1958, p. 11.

For 381 days, from Dec. 5, 1955, until Dec. 20, 1956, Montgomery's Negro citizens abandoned the city's segregated buses in a massive protest. A local seamstress, Rosa Parks, sparked the boycott when she was arrested after refusing to give up her seat to a white man.

The leaders of the Negro community quickly formed the Montgomery Improvement Association (MIA) to organize and lead the boycott. They turned to a young, largely unknown local pastor, the Rev. Dr. Martin Luther King, Jr., of the Dexter Avenue Baptist Church, to head the MIA.

The rest is history. Dr. King quickly emerged as a local and national figure in the civil rights movement and guided the boycott to a successful conclusion.

Janet Bell, a reporter at the *Observer*, told the story of the boycott in her 1957 book, *381 Days: The Story of the Montgomery Bus Boycott*. In a new memoir, *Stride Toward Freedom: The Montgomery Story*, Dr. King tells the story from the vantage point of the ramparts.

Dr. King is obviously the focal point of the story, but he is quick to share credit. The story, he writes, is "the chronicle of 50,000 Negroes who took to heart the principles of nonviolence, who learned to fight for their rights with the weapon of love, and who in the process, acquired a new estimate of their own human worth."

The basic story told in Bell's and Dr. King's accounts line up fairly consistently. The most obvious divergence is the inside knowledge that Dr. King brings to the narrative, and he uses that information to considerable dramatic effect, especially when discussing the boycott's impact on his family and his mental health.

Stride Toward Freedom has garnered favorable reviews from around the country, and sales are brisk. Dr. King has held several book signings at local churches, and the response has been overwhelming. John Ales, a member at Dexter Avenue, praised the book as a faithful account of the boycott. "What I read is what I saw, and I saw most of it," he said.

Robert Ball, another Dexter Avenue parishioner, said that while Dr. King had earned his new prominence, he was afraid that Dexter Avenue might lose him. "He's already taken on the leadership of the Southern Christian Leadership Conference, so he's on the road a lot. I'm afraid that he'll outgrow us."

Bell and Dr. King should have even more competition soon. Alabama State University professor, Lawrence D. Reddick, who assisted Dr. King in writing *Stride Toward Freedom*, is said to be completing a biography on Dr. King that is scheduled for a 1959 release.

****

"Ribbons," by Joel Stewart, *Alabama Magazine*, December 2009, pp. 4-5.

I've been competitive for as long as I can remember. I can't say exactly where that fire came from, though; certainly not from my dad who frowned on Type A behavior. Why, he once wondered out loud, were we fertilizing the grass? The faster it grows, the more often it needs to be cut. Nature is fertile enough. No need to encourage it.

Don't get me wrong. My dad did what needed doing at work and at home. He just didn't believe in overdoing it. He actually enjoyed his job, but he didn't recommend it to us kids. No, he tried to steer us toward teaching school or working for the government. You won't get rich, he conceded, but you're not likely to get fired or work yourself into an early grave.

I kept it to myself, but I always had high expectations. I wanted to win at everything: baseball, spelling bees, and checkers.

Dad often looked at me like he couldn't figure out where I came from.

At Sunday School, we often played a game called "Bible Drill." The object was to be the first to find a particular verse in the Bible. We held our closed Bibles in front of us, and the teacher would call out a verse: "John 3:16." We'd frantically flip through the pages until someone found it.

I don't know what, if any, ecclesiastical goal the drill accomplished, but I took it seriously. Well, I took winning it seriously. So seriously that I memorized the books of the Bible—Old Testament and New—in order; anything to secure an advantage.

So, when our sixth-grade teacher, Mrs. Mathews, announced that we were going to play a grammar game—and for grades—I was all in, or so I thought.

On that Monday morning, Mrs. Mathews gave each of us a ribbon to wear on our shirt or blouse. Over the coming week, we would have to forfeit the ribbon if a fellow student caught us in a grammatical error: dangling participles, split infinitives, using the ubiquitous, but deadly "ain't." The object was to collect as many ribbons as possible since your grade on the exercise depended on it.

The idea was to promote proper grammar among a demographic for which the term redneck was invented. We were not just country. We were Deep South country. For us, second person singular and plural was "y'all." Lie was lay, may was can, and never the twain shall meet.

I was a redneck too, but I was determined not to be one forever. So, I read everything I could get my hands on and did all of the homework assigned and more. I also had an excellent memory for facts and figures, so grammar rules weren't a problem.

This was going to be more fun than a possum hunt, and about as genteel. The whole exercise, you see, was self-policed. If you caught a classmate in a mistake—"Let's go in the room"—you pointed out their error and asked for their ribbon. Problems arose when there was no other witness to the verbal faux pas, and the miscreant refused to acknowledge her error. Voices were raised, feelings hurt, and friendships tested. Who knew?

Some students refused to play, sacrificing their ribbon early and withdrawing from further competition. They were the same ones who seldom did their homework and never answered questions in class. The ones that the teachers largely ignored as long as they kept quiet. Theirs was a Faustian Bargain that left students poorer.

A few simply refused to speak unless it was absolutely necessary, and even then, they proceeded carefully. I thought such a tactic violated the spirit of the exercise, if not the rules.

There were other problems as well. The competition wasn't fair. Some of the kids had no chance. That's a fact and they knew it. That's why they gave up so readily and feigned contempt for the rest of us grubbing after pieces of colored cloth. Almost from the start, I wondered if this was a good idea for anyone, even me.

That first morning, I took a ribbon from a classmate who made such an egregious error that I couldn't resist. He seemed relieved to be rid of the thing, but that didn't make me feel any better. In fact, I felt like an intellectual bully, and I've never liked bullies of any sort.

There was worse to come. Later that Monday, I caught my best friend, James Morgan, in a mistake. I don't think that he was even aware of it, and I had a split-second decision to make. Call him out or keep quiet. I chose to keep quiet. James kept his ribbon. I learned that competition has its limits.

I ended the week with three ribbons: the one I began with, the one I took almost by default that first day, and a third that I gladly took from the teacher's pet. Others had more, but most had less. I had just the right number for me.

Joel Stewart, former City Editor at the *Birmingham Star-Ledger*, is a contributing editor for *Alabama Magazine* and the author of *Crimson Voices: An Oral History of Alabama Football*. He grew up in Grover's Fork, Alabama, surrounded by cotton fields.

CHAPTER 13
GREAT MAN THEORY

"Buddy Holly Dead in Iowa Plane Crash," by Lee Allman, *The Wiregrass Herald*, February 4, 1959, p. 2.

(SPA) Clear Lake, Iowa. Rock and Roll lost three of its brightest stars when their chartered plane went down in a snowstorm near this northwest Iowa town. Artists Buddy Holly, Richie Valens, and J.P. Richardson (the Big Bopper) died in the crash along with Roger Peterson, the plane's pilot.

The three musicians had played at Clear Lake, Iowa's, Surf Ballroom on the evening of February 2 as part of their Winter Dance Party tour across the Midwest. The tour traveled by bus, but on this occasion, Holly abandoned the bus and chartered a four-seat Beechcraft Bonanza to fly him and two of his band mates to Fargo, North Dakota, for their next scheduled date in nearby Moorhead, Minnesota.

According to a source in the Cerro Gordo County Sheriff's office, Waylon Jennings and Tommy Allsup from Holly's band gave up their seats on the flight to Valens and Richardson. The same source told SPA that neither Peterson nor his employer, Dwyer Flying Services, was certified to fly in weather that required Instrument Flight Rules.

Peterson took off at 12:55 a.m. on Feb. 3 despite the inclement weather and crashed in a cornfield shortly after takeoff.

The 22-year-old Holly's ("Peggy Sue," "That'll Be the Day," "Rave On") rise was meteoric, and he seemed destined for a brilliant career as a singer and songwriter. Seventeen-year-old Valens began his brief career in 1958 and made the charts with "Donna" and "La Bamba." Richardson, 28, was best known for his 1958 hit "Chantilly Lace."

The investigation into the crash continues, but officials say that early results suggest pilot error was a factor. Peterson was a relatively inexperienced pilot and was only certified for flights using Visual Flight Rules.

****

February 14, 1959

Dear Janet,

I'm sure you saw the news about Buddy Holly. It's so sad. James took the news hard. Just in the months before the accident, he had been listening less to Elvis and more to Buddy. Military service has slowed down the Elvis juggernaut, but only somewhat. His label keeps releasing records even while Private Presley is stuck somewhere in Germany.

What struck me was how young those boys were. Holly was twenty-two and Richie Valens was only seventeen. Why wasn't he in school? He's traveling the country for months with a rock and roll tour, and he's only four years older than James. How is that possible? I've heard his hit song "Donna" on the radio and like it, but I never imagined he was so young.

I guess it makes some sense: Rock and roll is about the young, right? But still, seventeen? We had to be in before midnight, and that was on the weekend. And forget about going out on school nights unless it was a school event. Even at Birmingham-Southern, we had to be in the dorm by midnight on Friday and Saturday, ten on weeknights.

My own teenager—that still gives me pause—is beginning to act like a teenager. He's not nearly as agreeable as he was just last year. His favorite phrase is, "Aw Mom," and he screws up his face when I kiss him. At least he doesn't turn his head. I know it's normal, but that doesn't make it any easier. Maybe I should see what Dr. Spock has to say about the teenage years. I'm sure that I still have the book, but I haven't looked at it for years. How have I managed?

At least James doesn't seem to have noticed the girls yet. I don't know how I'm going to handle his puberty. I handled mine badly. What about "the talk"? That could be interesting. Maybe there's a book for that. I know one thing for certain: I don't want Ernest to do it. I don't know what, if anything, he told Roger about the birds and the bees, but I swear that he was less prepared for the marital bed than I was.

Mom simply told me that sex was a sin unless you were married. She just assumed that I didn't want to sin. As for my wedding night, she said that my husband would know what to do. I wondered if premarital sex was only a sin for women, but I didn't dare ask. I'm going to tell James the truth if I figure it out in time.

I probably don't need to worry about Ernest meddling. He has his own problems. He might have won reelection, but his critics haven't gone away. Now, it appears that the *Herald* has joined the chorus. Just last week, they ran a story questioning the commission's decision to delay the reconstruction of Highway 69 for another year. Most of the north- and south-bound traffic for the new hospital will use 69. Ernest insists that the commission has to make tradeoffs and some of the county's farm-to-market roads are in worse shape. Of course, the majority of his support comes from the people who depend on those rural roads.

Let's face it: He's fighting a rearguard action, and I think he knows it. The future is Centerville; Grover's Fork and the other small towns and crossroads villages have to adapt or die. I love Grover's Fork, but I'm not going to wax sentimental about it.

History doesn't care about Grover's Fork any more than it cared about Babylon. It follows the path of least resistance. The smart thing to do is to get on board and ride it to your final destination. Why make the journey any harder than it has to be? The last thing you want to do is stand in its path.

Listen to me! I sound like Dr. Green talking about Henry Adams. Remember the "arrow of time"? Always moving inexorably forward toward a fixed destination, pulled along by the masses. It appealed to me more than either the Great Man theory or Marx's foolish disregard for human nature.

On the final exam in intellectual history, I added a P.S. to my answer about the Great Man theory: Something to the effect that there's no Great Woman theory because women know the perils of hubris. Dr. Green must have agreed. I got an A.

Anyway, the masses have decided that cities represent opportunity and excitement, and they're voting with their feet. Ernest can't stop them. When we were growing up, Grover's Fork was still a bustling market town. In another decade, it'll be a quaint shell of its former self, long on nostalgia and short on hope. I'm happy that James is growing up here, but I'd be disappointed if he came back after college.

On that cheery note, I should go. But not before I say…

Happy Valentine's Day!
Mildred

****

February 21, 1959

Dear Mildred,

Your last letter got me thinking about Rev. King. I think that Henry Adams would agree that history makes the man, not the opposite. If I recall, Dr. Green used several examples to demonstrate the point: Martin Luther, Napoleon Bonaparte, and of course, Thomas Jefferson from Adams' *History of the United States, 1801-1817*.

Luther exploited the church's vulnerability after centuries of ecclesiastical abuse, and Bonaparte seized upon the possibilities that the French Revolution presented. Neither actually "made" the historical movements that they led. That doesn't mean that they weren't important. It does mean that they weren't the World Historical Figures that many make them out to be.

The Jefferson example is entirely different. Luther and Napoleon saw which way history wanted to go and used their considerable talents to expedite it. Jefferson, on the other hand, misread history's mind and tried to steer it in another direction. Even with the power of the presidency behind him, he failed. History moved steadily away from his ideal of America as a nation of yeoman farmers. His primary rival, Alexander Hamilton, correctly identified the way forward: manufacturing, trade, and cities.

So, as for Dr. King: The bus (sneaky metaphor) was already leaving the station when he was asked to take the wheel. There can be no doubt that he's a capable, articulate, and charismatic leader. But I don't think there's any doubt that the movement is making him, not vice versa. Yes, he's providing visibility and energy, but let's not forget that Rosa Parks came first.

Personally, I'm not comfortable with the people most closely associated with a heroic view of history: Hegel, Spengler, and Nietzsche. Especially Nietzsche. I'm also not a fan of many of the so-called Great Men. Most of them as you know—Luther and

Bonaparte are blatant examples here—are misogynists. Maybe that's what makes a Great Man. The one thing that I'll never forget from Western Civ is the example from "Luther's Table Talk" that Dr. Stringer cited: God made women with big behinds so that they could stay home and sit on them. I'm sure that Mrs. Luther got a chuckle out of that.

As for Napoleon, you know how much I appreciate neurotic, short men. I realize that's not fair to most short men, but it's the bad actors that we remember. Bonaparte has his champions of course, but I doubt that many of them are women. I once wrote this Napoleonic quotation on a 3x5 card that I still have: "The weakness of women's brains, the instability of their ideas … their need for perpetual resignation … all this can be met only by religion." How could any self-respecting woman have slept with this man?

Listen to me. Dick Hadley once told me that I'm much too serious. And that I scared away all the young men. Imagine that? Scary me. He traced it to Birmingham-Southern. He said that if I had gone to Alabama, I'd spend less time pondering the meaning of things and more time accumulating things. Of course, he went to Birmingham-Southern too. So, maybe I was damaged goods before I arrived at college. What do you think? Be careful here. You have always been the one most likely to overthink things. Weren't you voted that in high school?

I too was surprised to find out how young Buddy Holly and Richie Valens were. Aren't musicians supposed to have to pay dues before they become famous? Seventeen! Most nights at seventeen I was in bed by 10:00. I had to beg to borrow the car to drive downtown. Forget about driving to Centerville alone. Ten miles away and it might as well have been on the moon. Maybe you grow up faster in Lubbock, Texas, than in Grover's Fork, but I doubt it. I looked Lubbock up in a road atlas, and it's more isolated than the Wiregrass.

That reminds me … I was in the drugstore one day when we were in high school, and I heard a farmer say that he didn't live at the end of the world but that he could see it from his porch. The image created quite an impression on me. In retrospect, he was obviously making a joke, but it sounded so lonely to me. For once, I was happy that I lived in Grover's Fork and not way out in the country.

Tell James hello and to keep practicing his guitar. I'm not so serious that I don't enjoy a little rock and roll now and then.

Love,
Janet

****

October 4, 1959   *The Wiregrass Herald*   A14

OBITUARIES

U.S. Army Captain Luke Michaels of Tall Pines, North Carolina, and a native of rural Wiregrass County died on September 26 while serving as an advisor to the Army of the Republic of Vietnam's 23rd Division. A member of the Army's First Special Forces Group, Michaels was mortally wounded when a large insurgent force ambushed the 23rd Division. Michaels was slated to return to Ft. Bragg, North Carolina, this month.

Capt. Michaels was born in Centerville, Alabama, on July 18, 1929, and grew up in rural Wiregrass County. He graduated from Wiregrass County High School in 1947 and Auburn University in 1951. He was commissioned a second lieutenant in the Army upon graduation from Auburn. Michaels is survived by his wife, Mandy Jean (nee Price), and daughter, Sarah Elizabeth of Tall Pines; parents, John and Lawanda Michaels, of Centerville; and brothers, Mark and Jeffrey. Funeral arrangements are pending.

****

October 9, 1959

Dear Janet,

I doubt that you knew Luke Michaels, but I'm sending his obituary from the *Herald*. I didn't know him until I returned after college. He entered the high school in 1943, so he was a sophomore when I started as librarian. He was such a nice boy. Hard-working and smart. I knew that he'd go places. I just never imagined that he'd go someplace like Vietnam.

When I saw the obituary, I was beyond surprised. I had to look Vietnam up in an atlas. My only thought was, why was Luke in Vietnam? So, I put on my reference librarian hat and checked *The Reader's Guide*. And guess what, we're there containing communism. It's another North/South thing like Korea. I know that I'm no expert on national security, but nothing about Vietnam looks particularly threatening to me. All I can think is, *Doesn't anybody remember Korea?* That was only five years ago. If I recall, it was a bloody mess.

To be honest, I'm also worried about James. He'll be eighteen in four years and eligible for the draft. I have no problem with him serving, but I don't want him fighting somebody else's war. I know from the articles I found that the Army's current role in Vietnam is advisory only, but what happens if that's not enough to defeat the insurgents? Do we admit our mistake and get out? Or do we double-down to save face? I don't want the Department of Defense saving face on the back on my boy.

I know we're not perfect, but I still love our country, but more and more, I wonder what's being done in our name that we're not told about. Maybe I should have known that we had advisors in Vietnam, but I didn't. When did we debate this? Anyway, why am I writing you about this? I should write my congressman and the editor at the *Herald*. It probably won't do any good, but it's better than nothing, right?

Other than getting upset about Luke Michaels and Vietnam, things have been quiet here recently. Joel turned fourteen last month and started working part-time at the picture show, so he has less time for James. Joel's dad is doing what he can to keep the picture show going. The entire family now helps out selling tickets, working concessions, or cleaning up. I believe that other than family, there's only one employee left. That saves quite a bit. Even so, I'm not sure how much longer he can keep it going.

We take things for granted, and then we're surprised when they're gone. I certainly can't point fingers. I almost never go anymore. Back when we were in school, we often went twice a week, more in the summer. I blame television. It's made us so lazy. We'll miss the picture show when it's gone. The town will be diminished in some way.

Aren't I the jolly correspondent tonight? Sorry. I guess that I should get out more. School, supermarket, church, and repeat. That's a life? Don't answer that. I'm married, but I have no husband. I have no husband, but I'm not divorced or widowed. Legally, Roger won't be dead for another four years. It doesn't matter really. Once burned, twice shy. James is my port in the storm, but he'll be gone before I know it. Actually, he's already gone in some ways. I guess that's part of my morose mood. What a descriptive word morose is. It sounds just like it feels.

I'd better go before I have you in tears.

Morosely yours,
Mildred

****

"Rev. King to Leave Montgomery for Atlanta," by Earl Thomas, *The Montgomery Observer*, November 30, 1959, p. 1.

After weeks of rumors, the Rev. Dr. Martin Luther King, Jr. submitted his resignation to Dexter Avenue Baptist Church yesterday. He is moving his family to Atlanta where he will join his father at Ebenezer Baptist Church.

Rumors have swirled since King was named president of the Atlanta-based Southern Christian Leadership Conference (SCLC), a civil rights organization focused on using nonviolent direct action to challenge segregation. The SCLC grew out of the 1955-56 Montgomery Bus Boycott and the Montgomery Improvement Association (MIA) that guided it. King vowed to remain an active member of the MIA.

King assured his local followers that he wasn't abandoning them. "I hate to leave Montgomery," he said, "but the people here realize that the call from the whole South is one that cannot be denied."

King revealed that the SCLC was planning a "south-wide" campaign and that "Atlanta is perhaps the most strategic location for the headquarters of this expedition."

One of the oldest members at Dexter Avenue echoed King's statement: "Rev. King will not truly be leaving us because part of him always will remain in Montgomery, and at the same time, part of us will go with him."

See "King," p. 4

****

December 2, 1959

Dear Mildred,

I'm sure that you saw the news: Dr. King is moving to Atlanta. He has clearly outgrown Montgomery, and we knew that it was just a matter of time before he left. Even so, it'll take a bit of getting used to. Rev. Abernathy is still here, though, and he's long been Dr. King's right-hand man in the Montgomery Improvement Association, so it's not like there's a leadership vacuum left behind.

Earl Thomas asked if I regretted not taking the job at the *Constitution* now that Dr. King is moving to Atlanta. It's a fair question. I don't think so. I still believe that a successful civil rights movement has to come through Alabama. So, I still believe that I'm in the right place at the right time. Is it wrong of me to be thinking about my career here? Sometimes, I wonder. But—rationalization alert—this history will happen with or without me. Somebody needs to cover it. Why not me, right?

Martha Gellhorn, one of my heroes, made her fame and fortune covering wars. Somebody else made the wars. Why should she have to apologize for doing a hard, dangerous job very well?

Yes, I'm ambitious. Always have been. You know that as well as anyone. I didn't just want to be a journalist. I wanted to be a famous journalist. I worked hard to become a good reporter and writer, and I've been fortunate to land in the middle of perhaps the biggest domestic story of the decade.

I'm not the bad guy. I'm for justice. Not that history cares anything about justice. Anybody who believes that doesn't know much history. But in this case, history seems to be slouching toward justice. It's a compelling story, and the fact that justice and my ambitions are aligned shouldn't matter. At least, that's my story and I'm sticking to it.

Did James listen to the Iron Bowl? Alabama fans must be quite happy with their choice of Coach Bryant. It was beginning to look like they would never beat Auburn again. Everybody expected good things from Coach Bryant, but I don't think anybody expected such a quick turnaround. I'm looking forward to the Liberty Bowl game with Penn State. The teams seem to match up well—yes, I've been listening to the sports reporters—and it should be competitive. NBC is televising the game, so you should be able to get it on WHOD.

I can't believe that Christmas has come around again so soon. I'll be happy to have some time off to visit, but I'm not ready for Christmas shopping. Any ideas about what I can get James? Teenage boys are too old for toys, but not old enough for clothes, right? Any help will be appreciated.

Bye,
Janet

****

"Penn State Edges Alabama in First Liberty Bowl," by Larry Ellis, *The Wiregrass Herald*, December 20, 1959, p. C1.

The Penn State Nittany Lions spoiled the Alabama Crimson Tide's first bowl trip since 1955 with a 7-0 win in the inaugural Liberty Bowl.

The game, played in cold, windy conditions at Philadelphia Municipal Stadium was a defensive struggle from start to finish. The Nittany Lions (8-2), coached by Rip Engel, scored the game's only touchdown on a fake field goal attempt.

Alabama (7-1-2) Coach Paul Bryant refused to use the inclement weather as an excuse. "We were out-blocked, out-tackled, and out-coached," Bryant told the press after the game.

While the Alabama defense acquitted itself well, the offense hardly showed up, and the kicking game often left the Tide with poor field position. Penn State's lone touchdown came near the end of the first half following a four-yard Alabama punt that set the Nittany Lions up deep in Alabama territory. Penn State ran a couple of plays before setting up for the fake field goal, which led to an 18-yard touchdown pass.

When asked, Bryant admitted that the fake kick surprised his defenders. "It certainly did. It was a well-executed play that fooled us. They did it beautifully."

See Liberty Bowl, p. C2

CHAPTER 14
LOOKING FORWARD

"Top 10 Fearless Predictions for the 1960s," by Mack Jones, *The Wiregrass Herald*, January 1, 1960, p. 5.

If you've gotten this far into today's paper, you've probably read our New Year's editorial. If you skipped it on your way to the Sports page, go back and take a look. The paper's editorial board surveys the past decade and finds much to like, and with good reason. Despite some stumbles, the 1950s were much more prosperous and peaceful than the two previous decades of depression and war. Looking ahead, we expect more of the same from the 1960s.

So, we're optimistic here at the *Herald*, but we also wanted to know what our readers are seeing in their crystal balls. To find out, we asked ten local leaders representing government, business, agriculture, and education for their predictions for the coming decade. The answers might surprise you. Some of them also might be right.

10. "The University of Alabama will win a national championship under Coach Bryant who will then leave to coach in the NFL."—Jack Olden, Head Football Coach, Centerville High School

9. "Coach Bryant will prove to be a flash-in-the-pan at Alabama, and Shug Jordan's Auburn Tigers will dominate the 1960s."—Morris Black, Head Football Coach, Chattahoochee Valley High School

8. "We learned an important lesson from Korea. It will be our last war of containment."—Dr. Brad Martin, Professor of Political Science, Troy State College

7. "The FDA will approve an oral birth control pill, and the post-war surge in births will finally come to an end. That's the easy part. The harder part is figuring out the relationship between a readily available pill and pre-marital sex. I'm guessing that we're in for a sexual revolution."—Dr. Leonard Jackson, Wiregrass County Hospital

6. "Vice President Nixon will be elected president in 1960 and will continue the successful policies of President Eisenhower."—Jean MacArthur, Chairman of the Wiregrass County Republican Party

5. "All Alabama schools will be integrated this decade. The politicians will declare victory and move on."—Rev. Joseph Waters, African Methodist Episcopal Church of Centerville

4. "Rock and roll will be a passing fad. This latest generation of kids will turn out to be more interested in conformity than rebellion."—Brad Connors, Principal, Centerville High School

3. "People will continue to move from farms and small towns to larger urban areas. Industry will grow in importance, and agriculture will shrink. That will worsen the divide between Centerville and the rest of the county."—Mel Adams, Director, Centerville Chamber of Commerce

2. "Jim Folsom will win his third term as governor in 1962, narrowly defeating George Wallace."—Lee Holman, Chairman of the Wiregrass County Democratic Party

1. "George Wallace will be Alabama's next governor. I know that it's early, but I'm endorsing him today. He'll fight for the people of Alabama."—Ernest Morgan, Chairman, Wiregrass County Board of Commissioners

****

March 16, 1960

Dear Janet,

Looks like summer has come early to the Wiregrass; just in time for Spring Break, I guess. I've spent most of the break cleaning house and reading. James has been in and out all week, but mostly out. He and Joel ride their bikes all over town. They usually take their baseball gloves with them, so I assume they're playing ball.

Listen to me: "I assume." He's fourteen, so I have to give him some freedom, but I still worry. At least it's Grover's Fork. How much trouble can he get into? I'd be stricter if it was Montgomery. I can't even imagine beyond that, like Birmingham or Atlanta? I just hope that I'm not underestimating how much trouble a teenager can find in a little place like Grover's Fork.

Speaking of trouble: Ernest wants James to work at the farm again this summer. This time without Joel who's now working at the picture show. James is all for it. He's saving to buy a new guitar and an amplifier, so he needs the money. He knows that his grandpa will overpay him. What's not to like? It's so obvious that Ernest hopes that James will join him one day and keep his legacy intact. It's a tarnished legacy though, and his own sons knew it. I've just got to trust that James will see it too.

The *Herald* continues to probe the dealings of the County Commission, but it's all conjecture and appearances. Lots of smoke but no fire so far. I don't know if I mentioned it before, but Ernest has already endorsed Wallace for governor two years early. I thought that was strange. In fact, I don't recall him endorsing anyone before.

I don't think that Ernest is a racist. He just doesn't like anybody. He tolerates people who are useful to him, but nothing more, which includes me, James, and maybe even Helen. I know that sounds awful, right? But I've never seen him show her any affection.

So, what is this endorsement about? Obviously, he thinks that Wallace can be helpful to him. It's clear—at least to me—that all the trends—demographic, economic, and social—are running contrary to Ernest's best interests. So he's looking for a way to hold on to power. The race card is a convenient one to play. Wallace thinks it will work, and Ernest apparently agrees.

I don't know if Ernest thinks Wallace can win the governor's race, but he apparently believes that Wallace can carry Wiregrass County. So he's planning to ride his coattails to reelection. Seriously, Ernest doesn't care what happens beyond Wiregrass County.

I say that, but he did mention the presidential election at dinner last Sunday. He admits that Senator Kennedy will appeal to many voters, but he thinks that the majority will be more comfortable with Vice President Nixon, substance over style. In Ernest's folksy idiom, Kennedy is "all sizzle and no steak."

I'm not so sure that voters will agree. Anyway, after eight years of Ike, a little sizzle might be a good thing. I know that it's not supposed to matter, but I know lots of women who find Kennedy very attractive, me included. Plus, Nixon seems to be wound too tight. Now that I think about it, he reminds me a lot of Ernest. I guess that decides it: I'm voting for Kennedy.

Do you think the sit-in movement will reach Montgomery? It looks like a piece with Rev. King's agenda of non-violence. It's also the best way to seize the moral high ground. Violence will scare people and push them away. I know that it would frighten me, and I'm sympathetic.

I read a few days ago that we're sending another 3,500 soldiers to Vietnam. It was just a couple of paragraphs in a news summary tucked away inside the paper. I wouldn't have thought anything about it except for the death of Luke Michaels last fall. There's a war in Vietnam, we're getting more involved, and nobody seems to be paying much attention.

Of course, I'm taking it personal. James is another year closer to the draft. I've been reading whatever I can find on Vietnam, and I'm not encouraged that we know what we're doing over there. It's like Korea has been forgotten already. If James has to go to war, I'd like for it to mean something.

Okay, my rant's over. I just feel so helpless. Anyway, I'm probably overreacting. My dad used to say, "Don't buy trouble." I think he meant that it would find you soon enough, so don't go looking for it. I just wish that I could trust our politicians not to go looking for trouble.

On a happier note, is there any chance that I'll see you over Easter?

Love,
Mildred

****

August 1, 1960

Dear Mildred,

Well, I finally read Harper Lee's novel this past weekend. I'm not sure what I think about it, to be honest. It's like two books in one: The mystery of "Boo" Radley and the drama of Tom Robinson's rape trial. Lee makes it work, but it's not a smooth fit. That's not to say that I didn't enjoy it. I did. Very much. She certainly shines a light on the corrosive effect of racism on our communities.

From what I've seen, the reviews have been good and the sales better. You know that she attended Huntingdon before going to law school at Alabama? So, that's a bragging point for them. The novel is somewhat autobiographical. The three young children in the book are based at least loosely on Harper, her brother, and their childhood friend, Truman Capote, who spent several summers in Lee's hometown of Monroeville.

Earl Thomas did the review for the *Observer*, and he focused on the novel's coming-of-age/loss-of-innocence aspect. Maybe that was Harper's main intention, but I don't think so. Anyway, the book's early success suggests a broader appeal to me. Dick Hadley knows the Lee family and tells me that her publisher didn't have very high hopes for the book. But she certainly seems to have hit a nerve.

Did you watch any of the coverage of the conventions? I know that much of it is hokey, but I couldn't help myself. I must say that I was more impressed with Kennedy than Nixon. They couldn't have chosen two different running mates with Lyndon Johnson and Henry Cabot Lodge. I can see how Johnson potentially helps Kennedy in the South, but how does Lodge help Nixon? Governor Rockefeller might have helped Nixon in the Middle Atlantic States, but I doubt that a Nixon/Lodge ticket even carries Massachusetts.

It appears that Nixon will campaign on the issue of experience, but Kennedy has a lot going for him. He's photogenic, telegenic, articulate, and charismatic. I almost included young as another contrast with Nixon. Despite appearances, Nixon is only four years older. Anyway, after all the shades of gray over the past eight years, maybe we need some color in the White House. While Nixon might be many things, colorful isn't one of them.

So, I imagine that you won't be surprised to hear that I'm supporting Kennedy. Who knows if it'll matter? Alabama Democrats are putting up a slate of five electors pledged to Kennedy and six unpledged electors. The unpledged electors will be free to vote for Kennedy, Nixon, or someone else. Why do we always have to call attention to ourselves and not in a good way?

Oh, before I forget, congratulate James on the Pony League All Stars' success. It's not easy for teams from towns like Grover's Fork to advance when they have to play teams from cities like Centerville. To have made the district finals is no small accomplishment. At least in high school, Grover's Fork will compete against schools their size.

How has his summer work with Ernest gone? I know that you worry about Ernest's influence on him, but at least he's learning about hard work. That can't be a bad thing. Plus, I can't see Ernest having more influence on James than you. So, stay vigilant, but don't worry so much.

I love my job, but in a way, I envy all the free time you have in the summer. Some days, I'd like to call in sick and just relax in the hammock all day. I'll never get that billboard out on the highway into Grover's Fork that way, will I?

Enjoy the rest of your summer. Come visit for a couple of days. I'm sure Ernest will give James a few days off. Just let me know when.

Love,
Janet

****

"Kennedy Wins Presidency in Tight Contest," by Earl Thomas, *The Montgomery Observer*, November 9, 1960, p. 1.

Democratic Senator John F. Kennedy of Massachusetts narrowly edged incumbent Vice President Richard M. Nixon yesterday in the closest presidential vote since 1916. The 43-year-old Kennedy becomes the youngest person elected to the office and will be the second youngest, after Theodore Roosevelt, to serve as president.

Kennedy won the popular vote by a microscopic .17% and won only 22 states to Nixon's 26, but nevertheless carried the electoral vote by a robust 303 to 219. Kennedy polled well in the Middle Atlantic, Deep South, and Upper Midwest, while Nixon dominated from the Great Plains to the West Coast.

Public opinion polls throughout the fall had indicated a tight contest, and the results bore them out. Kennedy's surprising selection of Texas Senator Lyndon B. Johnson as his running mate appears to have paid off as the Democratic ticket carried Texas, Louisiana, Arkansas, Georgia, and the Carolinas.

Nixon's choice of Henry Cabot Lodge of Massachusetts as his running mate didn't appear to have added much punch to the ticket. The GOP lost Massachusetts and managed only twelve electoral votes in the northeast region.

See "Kennedy," p. 5

****

"Big League Dreams," by Joel Stewart, *Alabama Magazine*, March 2008, pp. 8-9.

Growing up, I never wanted to be a fireman or a cop.

I wanted to play first base for the Brooklyn Dodgers, like Gil Hodges, the best player never elected to the Hall of Fame.

My best friend, James Morgan, cheered for the Bronx Bombers, aka, the New York Yankees. The Yankees were Darth Vader before there was a Star Wars. James idolized Yankees' centerfielder, Mickey Mantle, and was sure that he'd grow up to replace Mantle in the Yankees' outfield.

What neither of us knew was that no one from Grover's Fork had ever played in the majors, nor the high minors. NO ONE. What can I say? Somebody has to be first. (Fifty years later, Grover's Fork is still waiting for its first major leaguer.)

I grew up in the Deep South in the 1950s when the Mason-Dixon Line and the 100th Meridian marked the southern and western boundaries of professional baseball. Fans in Border States like Virginia and Kentucky were at least within the orbit of major league teams. Virginia could claim the Washington Senators, although that was a recipe for perennial disappointment. Only the Ohio River separated Kentucky from the Cincinnati Reds.

Here in deepest Dixie, however, there wasn't a team within cheering distance, so we had our pick. Lots of locals favored the St. Louis Cardinals since Missouri was not considered alien territory like, say, New York, and we could pick up the Cards' radio broadcasts.

My dad rooted for the Cards. His favorite player—although long-since retired—was Dizzy Dean. Dizzy did color commentary—and he was nothing if not colorful—on CBS's *Game of the Week* on Saturday afternoons. I seldom missed a game, but Dad ran the local picture show, and Saturday was the busiest day of the week.

Dad usually left the house on Saturday morning by 10:00. The afternoon matinee—a double feature—started at 1:00 p.m. and ended around 5:00. Mom dropped off his supper around 5:30. The evening feature started at 7:00. We were in bed when he finally got home, so I usually watched the game with James, mostly over at his house since he didn't have any sisters to bother us. His mom always made popcorn and chocolate chip cookies. Who said baseball goes best with Crackerjacks?

As I said, I liked the Dodgers, and James liked the Yankees. That actually was a good thing since they were in separate leagues and didn't play unless they met in the World Series. That happened often in the 1950s, but our friendship always managed to survive the inevitable friction. It helped that we agreed not to watch together. The Yanks usually won, which made the Dodgers' win in the 1955 Series especially sweet.

My dad missed most of my games, and we seldom played catch in the backyard. I never thought that I was missing out on something special. Dad worked long hours. He was rarely home before midnight, but there was never any doubt that he loved us.

Anyway, adults weren't as involved in their children's lives back then. The local Little League field didn't have lights, and we played in the afternoon when most parents couldn't get away. Years later, I learned that Yankees Catcher Yogi Berra never played catch at home with his sons. Why? "That's what brothers are for," Yogi pointed out. I didn't have brothers, only a sister, but James and I spent countless hours over the years playing catch.

In retrospect, I think that youth sports were probably better without all the adults. We kids got to play without the added stress of parents with their own dreams. Errors could be made and forgotten, not rehashed over dinner. As an adult, I coached my son's Little League team, and the difference between the eras was striking. I liked the old Mudville better. It was a much less intense place.

When I was in fifth grade, my teacher made us write an autobiography. Yeah, go figure: one hundred words would just about do it. I wrote that I planned to play first base for the Dodgers and pasted Gil Hodges' baseball card to the page.

But reality has a way of intruding on dreams. My reality was the curveball. The older I got and the better the pitchers got, the less I hit. By high school, I barely hit enough to make the team. Finally, as a junior, I switched to track. It was one of the best decisions I ever made.

So, I needed a Plan B for my future dreams. I found it in writing. I'd always been a prolific reader, and I thought that writers were special. Not as special as baseball players, but more people make a living writing than playing baseball. In fact, I knew someone from Grover's Fork who was a successful writer: Janet Bell who was a friend of James' mother.

I majored in journalism in college and minored in English. I've enjoyed a modestly successful career as a journalist, and I've written a fairly popular book about Alabama football. Newspapers and television have interviewed me. I've done book signings, all the author things, and sometimes, I've had to pinch myself.

Looking back, I need to thank all the pitchers who made me look bad. I was never going to make it to Ebbets Field anyway. I wouldn't have found anything there anyway. The Dodgers fled to Los Angeles in 1958, and the stadium was razed in 1960. Move on kid. There's nothing to see here.

Joel Stewart, former City Editor at the *Birmingham Star-Ledger*, is a contributing editor for *Alabama Magazine* and the author of *Crimson Voices: An Oral History of Alabama Football.* He grew up in Grover's Fork, Alabama, surrounded by cotton fields.

CHAPTER 15
BEAR EVERY BURDEN

February 14, 1961

Dear Janet,

Happy Valentine's to my oldest and dearest friend. I got my usual number of Valentines: none, but that's okay. When Roger disappeared, I deliberately chose a path of celibacy, and now I own it. Next year, I'll (we'll) be forty. If I'm not over the hill, I'm near the crest. Not many men are looking for middle-aged widows. At least everyone assumes that I'm a widow. The reality is that whether Roger is alive or not, I'm a widow.

This is the first Valentine's that James has shown any interest in girls. I'm sure that he was interested before, but he would never admit it. Now, he doesn't even try to hide it. Right now, he's mooning over Mary Carpenter, Philip Carpenter's daughter. Didn't you go out with him? At least once? Well, his daughter is a real cutie and apparently smart as a whip. I know that they exchanged Valentines because Joel told me. James blushed when Joel let it slip, but he didn't deny it. Do you think that we should have "the talk"? I don't know who would be more embarrassed.

On the subject of relationships, Rev. Givens resigned from the First Baptist Church last weekend, but not publicly. He told the deacons on Saturday, and they informed the congregation on Sunday morning. It was apparently quite a shock for everyone. The word (rumor?) on the street is that he was caught in flagrante delicto with Martha Berry, the church secretary, by one of the deacons in his office in the church. Poor Martha. I wonder who's putting together this week's Church Bulletin?

It could be worse. Remember when Rev. Nelson was caught "counseling" a married woman and had to leave town? I remember that we Methodists were pretty smug about it. What is it about adultery that these Baptists don't understand?

Anyway, the Givens' have already left town. He'll probably find another church. Ernest said that Givens agreed to resign, and the deacons agreed to cover for him, passing the trash. Where's the morality in that?

That leaves Martha and her husband to face the music. I feel sorry for her husband. How can he face people? Fortunately, they don't have children yet. Nobody seems to have seen either of them since Sunday. He works in Centerville, so I wouldn't be surprised to see them move.

I continue with church mostly out of habit, and for James. I guess that makes me a hypocrite too. I don't care what James eventually decides to believe, but I don't want him branded as an infidel in his hometown. Truth be told, half of the people in the pews on Sunday morning are there for appearance, not for salvation.

James already has his doubts about what he hears in church, and I'm sure that those doubts will grow as he does. Wait until he takes biology and physics. I'll be happy if he follows a single commandment: Be kind to others. In my opinion, it covers just about everything.

While James was watching television tonight, I curled up with Emily Dickinson. A well-worn Christmas gift from a dear friend. You know who you are. I'm not convinced that Miss Emily couldn't have used some "counseling" herself. I find it interesting that she wasn't a churchgoer for much of her life. Remember her poem, "Some keep the Sabbath going to Church— / I keep it, staying at Home"? That'll be me someday soon.

Since it's Valentine's, I revisited *Wild Nights—Wild Nights!* Remember how we argued about its meaning in American Lit class? I still don't believe Miss Emily, reclusive spinster that she was, meant it in an erotic way. I'm no literary critic, but I think that she was looking for a symbolic port in a metaphysical storm. I'm still stumped by the meaning of the "Rowing in Eden" phrase though, but that's okay. Where's the fun of it once you've figured it all out?

This is getting long, but I wanted to ask your thoughts on President Kennedy's inaugural address. It certainly struck a chord with a lot of people, and it was beautifully done. Listening to it, I was taken by its idealism and apparent humility, but reading it later, I was struck by its swagger— "we shall pay any price, bear any burden, meet any hardship"—and its seeming appeal to blind nationalism—"ask not what your country can do for you; ask what you can do for your country." It sounds a lot like the old Stephen Decatur "my country, right or wrong" toast. I want to believe the best about the new administration, but I don't want James bearing some false burden in some forsaken place like Joe did in Korea.

The press has decided that the new administration represents a modern-day Camelot with the president as King Arthur and Jackie as Guinevere. It's a fantasy, of course, but it always was. It's harmless as long as we remember that.

Okay, I've sufficiently unburdened myself. Thank you for listening. You are listening, aren't you?

Happy Valentine's!
Mildred

****

May 26, 1961

Dear Mildred,

Sorry I haven't written for a while, but as I'm sure you know, we've been busy around here. Earl Thomas and I worked almost around the clock for a couple of days covering the Freedom Riders stop here. We expected trouble and were on hand to greet them at the bus station. We weren't the only ones. So was a mob of agitators who attacked the riders almost immediately. Several had to be hospitalized.

Dr. King was scheduled to make a speech the next night at Rev. Abernethy's church, but a mob laid siege to the church, throwing rocks and bricks through the windows. Dr. King appealed to Bobby Kennedy by phone, and Kennedy called Governor Patterson. The next morning, the Alabama National Guard arrived and dispersed the mob.

I think I got about two hours of sleep that night. But I felt the most alive that I've felt in months. Stories like this are why I do what I do. I still wrestle with that though. Sometimes I feel like a voyeur. Or, worse: a parasite. Benefitting from someone else's misery. Even so, I'm still drawn to such stories like a proton to an electron. Although as a journalist, I'm supposed to be neutral like a neutron. Forgive me, I couldn't help myself. We spent a lot of time and money getting educated. Might as well flaunt it occasionally.

Anyway, conflict is at the heart of a good story, right? Where would Homer be without the Trojans? The conflict would still happen whether I was there to cover it or not. I was always on the side of those who thought that a tree falling in the forest made a sound regardless of whether anybody was there to hear it. And Schrodinger's cat is dead whether I look in the box or not. So, there.

The Kennedys' intervened to prevent a larger tragedy in Montgomery, but I bet they're frustrated that this story is not going away. The Bay of Pigs was not a good start for them, but they had started to recover their footing with Alan Shepard's successful space flight.

JFK's pledge this week to put a man on the moon before the end of this decade should have been a public relations bonanza for the administration. Here and around the world. The violence in Montgomery didn't spoil that for them, but it did take some of the luster off. The timing of the announcement was certainly fortuitous for the administration. It moves the Bay of Pigs mess to the back of the paper and even nudges coverage of the Freedom Riders' ordeal beneath the fold.

I certainly understand the allure of the space program. I watched as transfixed as everybody else during Alan Shepard's short trip into space. It's exactly the kind of great adventure you'd expect from Camelot. I wonder though what would happen if we put the same kind of effort into solving the civil rights conundrum. Is it so much harder than putting a man on the moon?

School should be out soon. I kind of miss the old days when my life was determined by the school calendar. I wonder if Einstein was thinking about school time when he came up with the theory of relativity. It was always my experience that time slowed down when school was in session and sped up after the final bell rang. Now, there's a paradox. Shouldn't we want more school and less vacation if that's the case? Otherwise, we'll grow old faster. Is that what's happening to you? Ha!

You and James should visit when school's out. What are his plans for the summer? Is he playing baseball again? This summer will be Colt League, if I remember correctly. After that, it's American Legion ball, right? I imagine that he'll work for Ernest again. He's getting old enough now to do some real work.

You never said, but I'm guessing that he has his driver's permit by now. How's that going? That's not something that I miss about not having children. Actually, there's not a lot that I do miss about it. Probably later when I'm all alone in life, I'll miss the company. But surely you and James will still visit occasionally. Or will you just move me into a home and forget about me?

You will come, okay? Early June before it gets so darned hot in the city. Just for a weekend if James' baseball schedule or work is a problem.

Love,
Janet

****

August 4, 1961

Dear Janet,

The Dog Days are upon us and with a vengeance. August is the price we pay for those mild winter days when Yankees are stuck inside with sub-zero temperatures and blowing snow. If that's the alternative, I'll take the August heat and humidity.

Even so, it's draining. Every summer, I consider getting the house air-conditioned, but it's just so expensive. Fortunately, we have lots of shade to keep the sun off the house. Ernest had central air installed several years ago, and it is nice, especially at mealtime. But it's still a luxury for me.

Thankfully, James' baseball season is over. Fortunately, they played in a league over in Centerville where they have lights. Starting at 7:00 p.m. is a lot better than 2:00 p.m. It's still uncomfortable on a calm, muggy evening but better than sitting out in the afternoon sun. The kids don't seem to notice as much though. James has been working outdoors all summer at the farm, and he hardly ever complains. It helps that Ernest is overpaying him.

James has put together a band. He and Joel play guitar, and they've recruited a drummer and a keyboard player from the school band. They've been practicing for a few weeks now, and they don't sound half-bad.

Against all odds, I was hoping that James might give up football, so he'd have more time for the band, but that's not happening. He's already running a bit in the late afternoon to get in shape for football practice. He'll be on varsity this year, but he won't start; very few sophomores do, but he's excited. I'll just have to hold my breath until November.

James has spent the summer following Mickey Mantle and Roger Maris as they try to break Babe Ruth's homerun record. The first thing he looks for in the paper is the Yankees' box score. Mantle is his idol, but he's rooting for Maris too; just not quite as hard. Joel is a Dodgers fan, but he's caught up in the chase too. And yes, I've caught the fever too. Lord knows there's nothing exciting happening in Grover's Fork.

With school only a month away, I'm wondering where the time went. Two trips to Montgomery, a bunch of baseball games, and lots of books. Is that enough? I'll never get rich as a librarian, but I have plenty of time for my greatest passion: reading. That won't buy me air-conditioning, but it helps keep me sane. That's worth something.

Try to come down for Labor Day. Help me enjoy the calm before the storm.

Love,
Mildred

****

"Move Over Babe, Maris Belts #61," by Rex Joseph, *The Wiregrass Herald*, October 2, 1961, p. 9.

(SPA) New York. NY Yankees' slugger Roger Maris etched his name in baseball history with his 61st home run of the season yesterday at Yankee Stadium. In the 162nd and final game of the regular season, Maris drove a pitch from Boston Red Sox starting pitcher Tracy Stallard ten rows into the right-field stands to pass Yankees' Hall of Famer Babe Ruth's 34-year-old single-season record.

Maris and teammate, Mickey Mantle, chased the Babe's record throughout the summer with Mantle falling out of the chase in September when he was sidelined by injury. Mantle has spent his entire career in pinstripes and was the fan favorite to topple Ruth.

Down the stretch, many fans openly rooted against Maris, who came over to New York from Kansas City in a 1959 trade. With the record on the line, only 23,154 fans turned out on a nice Sunday afternoon for the finale.

The Yanks clinched the American League pennant and a spot in the World Series weeks ago, so yesterday's finale meant little outside of Maris' assault on the record book.

Yankees' starter, Bill Stafford (14-9), and relievers, Hal Reniff and Luis Arroyo, combined to shut out the Red Sox 1-0, the winning run coming on Maris' 4th inning home run.

The Yanks (109-53) now turn their attention to the World Series where they'll be matched up against the National League champion Cincinnati Reds (93-61). The Series kicks off at Yankee Stadium on Wednesday. Probable starters for the Series opener are Whitey Ford for the Yanks and Jim O'Toole for the Reds.

****

December 3, 1961

Dear Mildred,

I called Col. Deal (he's retired of course, but he'll always be Col. Deal to me) last week and we had lunch. See the sacrifices I make for you. Well, he was surprised that you were interested in Vietnam. He said that few Americans had any idea that we were engaged in Vietnam, or that such a place even existed.

He admitted that the 16,000 advisers being sent to Vietnam was a big number and that it caught him by surprise, but he doesn't think we need to worry. They're advisers, not combat troops. And he's convinced that the Pentagon hasn't forgotten the lessons of Korea.

Vietnam is even more exotic and ill-suited to American-style industrial war. And then there's China. The Chinese intervened in Korea when U.N. troops threatened to take up positions near their border with the North. Well, China and Vietnam also share a border.

His final point was that no one knows what victory in Vietnam would look like. That alone, he said, was a showstopper. I don't know about you, but he convinced me. So, quit worrying. James is not going to Vietnam. Or any place else other than college.

Thanks for loaning me *Catch-22*. I finished it in a couple of evenings. What a hoot. It's not just the military that's absurd though.

You've probably seen this kind of stuff at school. I know I've seen it at the newspaper. So it's universal. That's why it touches a nerve with people. I loaned it to a colleague at work, but I'll return it at Christmas.

I'm going to try to get a week off at Christmas. Dad's not doing so well, and I'd like to spend some extra time with him and Mom. And you and James too. I'd love to hear James and his band play too. Should I bring earplugs?

See ya soon,
Janet

****

"Chasing a Legend," by Joel Stewart, *Alabama Magazine*, September 2008, pp. 7-8.

In the beginning was Ruth, and the Babe remains the gold standard by which baseball greatness is measured. Maris and McGwire and Bonds might have eclipsed his single-season home run record, but they couldn't compete with the Babe in the public's imagination.

Ruth, despite his warts, was a legend in his own time. In death, he became baseball's Zeus. How could mere mortals, even those few capable of chasing his records, hope to measure up?

Of the three successful assaults on the single-season home run record, the public embraced only Mark McGwire's in 1998. Perhaps only McGwire, a modern-day Paul Bunyan who struck towering, majestic (Ruthian) drives, seemed a reliable heir to the legend. That, of course, was before the public knew about the steroids. Now, McGwire finds the gates to the Hall of Fame barred to him.

In 2001, Barry Bonds had the misfortune of coming along so close in McGwire's wake, and his reputation as a selfish player rankled many. But if Bonds' quest was met with much apathy, there was little rancor. Then, Bonds too was exposed as a fraud. Afterwards, as Bonds chased Henry Aaron's record for career home runs, the fans turned on him. And while Bonds ultimately claimed the record, many fans refuse to recognize it.

It's probably not a good idea to challenge the gods. McGwire and Bonds obviously forgot the fate of Sisyphus, or more recently, Roger Maris. Bonds and McGwire were frauds, but Maris was a gentleman and got his strength the old-fashioned way: hard work. Like Ruth, his drugs of choice were tobacco and alcohol. Neither exactly performance-enhancing.

Maris' work ethic, good deportment, and relatively clean living counted little for him in 1961, and his pursuit of Ruth engendered little besides rancor. Even the hometown fans didn't embrace him. Of course, he played in the Bronx in Yankee Stadium, The House That Ruth Built. Ah.

Maris' run at Ruth in 1961 was as improbable as it was rancorous. In 1961, he had been with the Yankees only a single season, and it mattered little that he had won the Most Valuable Player Award in his first year in pinstripes. New York fans already had their hero, and one with a Yankee pedigree.

Mickey Mantle had debuted in New York in 1951 as the heir apparent to Joe DiMaggio. Strong and lightning-fast, the young slugger hit prodigious tape-measure home runs. If anyone was going to surpass the great Ruth, it was supposed to be Mantle, not some journeyman interloper from Kansas City.

There were many that summer that didn't want anyone, including Mantle, to break the record. Old-timers and traditionalists argued that expansion had diluted the pitching, the ball was livelier, and the season was longer.

I knew Ruth at a considerable distance from the stories of old men and the pages of books. I was a child of the fifties, and

Mantle defined the sports hero of that decade, the last when baseball dominated the landscape. Millions of boys, including my best friend, James, idolized The Mick. I was a Dodgers fan, but I admired Mantle. That's how popular he was.

What we didn't know was the private Mantle. Back then, the press was more respectful of celebrities' privacy, and sportswriters usually kept quiet about Mantle's drinking and carousing. The Babe had yielded to similar temptations, but it only added to his colorful legacy. Mickey wouldn't be so lucky.

By 1961, I was fifteen and working at the movie theater that my father managed. I played Colt League baseball that summer, but baseball no longer consumed me. I was more interested in cars and music. So, early in the 1961 season, I paid little attention to the baseball news. It didn't help that the Dodgers had finished a mediocre fourth the previous year.

But events soon conspired to draw me back into baseball's orbit. With Maris and Mantle hitting home runs at a record pace, the press converged on the pair. The coverage was relentless, and while the two principals in the drama struggled to cope with the attention, the public couldn't get enough.

By July 4th, I was fully invested in the story. Unlike many who saw Maris as a villain, I cheered for both. So did James, but he leaned, heavily, toward Mickey.

The home run race seesawed back and forth throughout the summer and into September when Mantle was sidelined by a hip injury. With only Maris left in the chase, the press scrutiny intensified to the point that his hair fell out. Somehow, he endured the relentless pressure and broke the record on the last day of the season in front of a sparse Yankee Stadium crowd. I was happy for him. I thought that records were made to be broken.

I grew up and learned things about Mantle that I didn't want to know. Out of public view, he had done things that were decidedly not heroic. He was a drunk, a serial adulterer, and an absentee husband and father.

Eventually, time and experience taught me a broader view of heroism. Heroes are the people who do what's right (especially when it's unpopular, hard, or dangerous), not for profit or recognition, but because it's right. And they're more likely to be found playing catch with their kids down the block than splashing home runs into McCovey Cove.

Joel Stewart, former City Editor at the *Birmingham Star-Ledger*, is a contributing editor for *Alabama Magazine* and the author of *Crimson Voices: An Oral History of Alabama Football*. He grew up in Grover's Fork, Alabama, surrounded by cotton fields.

CHAPTER 16
THE FIGHTING JUDGE: ROUND 2

February 24, 1962

Dear Janet,

It's been quiet around here lately, so no news (or gossip for that matter) to report. The strange thing is that even when there's no news, there's usually plenty of gossip. I don't know if this is a good thing or a bad thing. Stay tuned.

The only excitement at school lately was John Glenn's space flight last week. Principal Lynch let us set up a TV in the library for students to watch the launch. These things are still nerve-wracking. I can't imagine what it'll be like when (if?) we get to the point of actually trying to send a man to the moon.

Some of the older people in town aren't sure that all this space travel is a good idea. Even Mom is a little skeptical, and she's usually open to most things. She's seen a lot of change in her life. She was a girl when the Wright Brothers made the first flight, so space travel is a lot to absorb. Heck, it's a lot for me to process too.

James and his band (they're calling themselves The North Street Band) played for the Valentine's Dance at the high school. They got $50 for the gig; not much but they were excited. Everybody says that it went well. They played all sorts of stuff but more rock and roll than anything else, lots of Buddy Holly and Elvis and even some Paul Anka songs that I really like. I'm happy that he's having fun with this, but I hope that's all it is: fun. They sound good ... for Grover's Fork.

Listen to me: Don't do this, don't do that. Don't become a starving musician. Don't become a rich farmer. I'm still angry with Ernest for giving James a car for his birthday. I should have put my foot down and forbid it, but James would have been heartbroken, and I'd have been the villain. Ernest knew exactly what he was doing. Checkmate. But I think that he underestimates James. James doesn't mind hard work and actually likes working on the farm, but I doubt that he wants to become a farmer, even if it means being the proprietor of Ernest's little Wiregrass County Empire.

As expected, Ernest has competition for County Commission Chairman. Jerry Ingram, a Centerville attorney, is campaigning actively throughout the county. Ernest isn't popular among Centerville's boosters or the editors at the *Wiregrass Herald*, but he's wily and more than willing to play hardball. His early embrace of Wallace, who's very popular locally, was clearly intended to pry a critical mass of Centerville's working-class voters away from Ingram. I wouldn't bet against him.

I wouldn't bet against Wallace either. As you've hinted in your reporting, Big Jim hasn't aged well politically. I like what I've seen of DeGraffenried, but Wallace seems inevitable. I'm afraid that the result will be another black eye for the state. We can't seem to get out of our own way.

I'll see you in the paper,
Mildred

****

"Wallace Tops DeGraffenried for Democratic Gubernatorial Nomination," by Lee Holman, *The Wiregrass Herald*, June 25, 1962, p. 1.

Former state legislator and circuit judge, George C. Wallace, decisively outpolled State Representative Ryan DeGraffenried, Sr. in Tuesday's Democratic primary runoff for governor. After losing to incumbent Governor John Patterson four years ago in a runoff, Wallace trounced DeGraffenried by a margin of 11%.

Wallace campaigned in 1958 as a moderate, but following his loss, recast himself as a staunch segregationist. The 37-year-old DeGraffenried, a Tuscaloosa attorney and twelve-year veteran of the Alabama House of Representatives, ran as a racial moderate.

The vote was not as close as many expected after the June 3 primary when moderates, DeGraffenried and former governor, Jim Folsom, polled over 50% of the vote between them. Since no candidate received a majority, a run-off between Wallace and DeGraffenried, who finished first and second respectively, was required.

The combative Wallace, who relishes being called "Alabama's Fighting Judge," promised voters during the campaign that he would stand up against outside demands to segregate Alabama institutions. On Tuesday, Alabama voters endorsed that message of defiance.

See "Wallace," p. 5

****

"Morgan Turns Back Challenger," by Lee Holman, *The Wiregrass Herald*, June 25, 1962, p. 1.

Long-time Wiregrass County Commission Chairman Ernest Morgan turned away a challenge from Centerville attorney, Jerry Ingram, in Tuesday's election. Morgan topped Ingram 59% to 41% in what many observers thought would be a tight contest.

Morgan, from rural Grover's Fork, relied on his rural and small-town base and a surprisingly strong showing in Centerville precincts to extend his two decades as Commission Chairman. Morgan's allies on the five-member Commission, Joe Joseph, Phil Willis, and Pete Smalley, ran unopposed. Jack Jones, a prominent Morgan critic, defeated Centerville realtor Mike Espers for the final Commission seat.

Morgan thanked his supporters and promised to continue working for "all of the county's residents," a clear message to those who argue that the Commission often ignores the needs of Centerville.

Ingram was subdued in defeat but refused to speculate on what went wrong. Centerville Chamber of Commerce president and Ingram supporter, Jesse Bruner, blamed Morgan's enthusiastic embrace of gubernatorial candidate, George C. Wallace. "We wanted the election to be about the future of Wiregrass County. Ernest wanted it to be about the past. He won this time."

See "Local Results," p. 5

****

August 10, 1962

Dear Mildred,

Sorry I haven't written lately. The trip to Albany set me back more than I imagined it would. But I couldn't pass up the chance to go. Earl Thomas and I drove over the day after Dr. King was jailed again. We thought that might represent a turning point in the protests. It did but not in the way the protesters expected.

The protest movement there was clearly faltering, and Dr. King was obviously trying to breathe life back into it by choosing to go to jail instead of paying a fine. It didn't work. The mayor took away that platform by quickly releasing him. We were told that someone paid his fine but not who that someone was. Now, Dr. King and the SCLC are getting some blowback, especially from critics within the Student Nonviolent Coordinating Committee that launched the Albany protests last fall.

In the end, it looks like little will change in Albany. At least for now. So, I guess the bottom line is that the Albany Movement failed, but it's probably more complicated than that. We'll just have to wait and see. In the end, Earl and I wrote up a long narrative account of what we witnessed during our visit. It was interesting but not very insightful. We simply couldn't agree on what the insights are.

While it wasn't exactly the story we hoped, we were still disappointed in Mac's decision to run it below the fold. Especially so since the lead story, complete with a sultry photo, was Marilyn Monroe's death. In fact, the paper has run a Marilyn story every day since she died on August 5.

I get it. She's a famous actress. Okay, an actress famous for being sexy. Former wife of Joe DiMaggio and Arthur Miller. Intimate of the Kennedy brothers. Her death is obviously a tragedy on some level, but it's all everybody's talked about this week. Why are we so taken with celebrities? That's not a rhetorical question. I'd really like to know.

I wonder if celebrity is ever a good thing. In a way, Dr. King is becoming a celebrity. That's not a criticism. I don't think he chose that role. He took a leadership role in the movement, and the press has made him a celebrity. Some would argue that's a good thing. It brings attention and publicity to the cause. It ensures that it stays in the public eye. Some in Albany felt that Dr. King came into town and hijacked their movement. Nobody wants to say it out loud, but there were whispers in the background. I've also heard through the grapevine that not everybody is enthralled with passive resistance as a tactic.

That's why I'm convinced that it's absolutely crucial that Dr. King stays at the helm of the movement. We've discussed this before. History isn't about justice or morality or value judgments of any kind. It's a process driven by the billions of individual decisions made every day. As such, history can change its mind. Slavery was fine for thousands of years. Until it wasn't. Segregation was fine in this country for a century. Until it wasn't.

So, segregation is doomed. With or without Dr. King. That's been evident since *Brown vs. Board of Education*, if not Truman's executive order desegregating the military. Politicians like Wallace are on the wrong side of history and will be swept aside. A leader on the right side of history can help manage the change and even shape the details. That's why Dr. King's leadership is important, in my opinion.

Desegregation can look a lot of different ways. Some better than others. The way we get there is important in determining what it looks like. I think that Dr. King's embrace of non-violence and his vision of a color-blind society are the best way forward. So, we'll see.

It looks like James Meredith's attempt to integrate Ole Miss will happen this fall. Earl and I are monitoring the situation and hope to convince Mac to let us cover it. I'm hoping for the best but expecting the worst. I still remember how stressful it was covering Autherine Lucy's abortive attempt to integrate Alabama. Yeah, I know. I shouldn't complain. Imagine how she felt.

Okay, enough about me. School is right around the corner. Is James going out for football again? If so, practice should begin soon. He's a junior, so I'm guessing that he should play more this year. Maybe start, right? I know football isn't your favorite activity, but it has some value. Let's go with the conventional wisdom: It teaches teamwork and promotes physical fitness. Let's not mention its role in testosterone control. I don't envy you living with all that pent-up testosterone. I'm assuming it's still pent-up. Ha.

If James is going to play, I'll try to get down for one of his games. Maybe homecoming. The last time I was there for homecoming was, what, two years ago? It was our 20th reunion. That was actually fun. I thought that the 10th was a bit tense, but the 20th was more relaxed. People weren't trying so hard. Twenty-five should be even mellower. I'm hoping by then that the city will have put up that billboard with my picture out on the highway. I gave up a normal life for that billboard.

It's getting late. I should go. Thank you again for listening to me. After all this time, I still don't have anyone here that I trust enough to tell them my innermost thoughts. I once thought that Dick Hadley was going to fill that role, but he up and got married. The new Mrs. Hadley put a quick end to our *tete-a-tetes*. Not that she needed to worry. Oh, well.

Enjoy the rest of your summer,
Janet

****

"Meredith Registers at Ole Miss Under Federal Protection," by Janet Bell and Earl Thomas, *The Montgomery Observer*, October 2, 1962, p. 1.

Following a day of violence that left two dead, James H. Meredith, a 29-year-old Air Force veteran, officially enrolled at the University of Mississippi yesterday. U.S. Marshalls accompanied Meredith as he became the first Negro to enroll at the 114-year-old institution.

Meredith followed a path familiar to other civil rights pioneers: A federal court order to desegregate followed by a governor's resistance. "No school will be integrated in Mississippi while I am your governor," Mississippi Governor Ross Barnett pledged.

The Fifth U.S. Court of Appeals on September 28 found Barnett in contempt and ordered him arrested if the Court's order was not carried out by October 2. Meanwhile, Attorney General Robert Kennedy dispatched U.S. Marshalls and other federal officers to Oxford.

On Saturday, September 29, Mississippi officials withdrew the State Highway Patrol from the university, and on Sunday, September 30, a white mob attacked the federal forces patrolling the campus. In the ensuing violence, two civilians were killed, and hundreds were injured. Roving mobs set fire to cars and vandalized university property.

The Kennedy Administration responded by deploying a federalized Mississippi National Guard and federal troops to restore order.

On October 1, federal Marshalls escorted Meredith across a tense campus to enroll for classes. The historic event proceeded without incident.

See "Meredith," p. 5

****

October 3, 1962

Dear Janet,

I saw your piece on Ole Miss in yesterday's paper. I always worry about you covering these things. They always seem to get out of hand, and nobody is safe, not even a Pulitzer Prize-winning reporter. I do admire you, but I can't help but worry about you.

Reading your reports from Oxford, I was reminded again how futile all this resistance is. The Supreme Court has ruled that segregation is unconstitutional. There is no higher appeal. Get over it. And Ike and JFK have shown that they will enforce the law when openly confronted. No governor can compete with that. The whole thing is absurd.

I actually try not to think too much about it. What can I do? I try to be kind to everyone. I try to teach James to be fair and open-minded. I even voted for DeGraffenried for all the good it did. I speak to the Negroes that I know, but I wonder what they're thinking. I hope they don't think I'm patronizing them. I don't pretend to understand their situation. Sometimes, I wonder if there'll ever be a genuine reconciliation. Integration is inevitable, but what will that mean in practice? I guess we'll find out.

James is excited that you're coming down for homecoming. Only nine more days! I guess you can say we're both excited. We play Junction City. Remember how much we hated them? I don't think we beat them the entire time we were in high school. Times have changed though. Grover's Fork should be favored this year. James and Joel are both starting; James at end and Joel at guard.

Ernest comes to all the games. He thinks that most activities are frivolous but not football. Go figure. I'm sure that he's opposed to James' music, but he doesn't say anything. If it had been Roger or Joe, he'd have ridiculed them. But he's still hoping to lure James into the business, so he's on his best behavior. I doubt that it'll be pretty when James finally flies the Morgan Farm coop. Until then, James is the golden grandchild.

James and his band are going to play at the homecoming dance. They're being paid $100. I don't think they've gotten more than $75 before. They'd play for free though. They like the attention and the girls. I volunteered (you were volunteered too) to be a chaperone for the dance, so we'll have an excuse to hear the band. I think you'll be surprised at how polished they've become.

I should go. We're really looking forward to seeing you!

Love,

Mildred

****

"Khrushchev Blinks; To Remove Nuclear Missiles from Cuba," by John Malloy, *The Wiregrass Herald*, October 29, 1962, p. 1.

(SPA) Washington, D.C. Soviet Premier Nikita Khrushchev issued a formal statement yesterday in Moscow pledging to dismantle and remove Soviet missiles from Cuba. The Kennedy Administration acknowledged that an agreement had been reached to end the weeklong standoff between the two nuclear powers.

In exchange for the Soviet promise to remove nuclear-armed missiles from Cuba, the U.S. pledged not to invade Cuba in the future. The U.S. Quarantine of Cuba that President John F. Kennedy announced on October 22 will remain in effect until the missiles have been removed.

The Missile Crisis began on October 16 when an Air Force U-2 spy plane captured images of ballistic missile sites being constructed in Cuba, ninety miles from the U.S. The world learned of the discovery six days later when Kennedy revealed the presence of the missiles in a televised address to the nation.

While denouncing the Soviets, the President ordered a Naval Quarantine of Cuba to prevent any additional offensive weapons from reaching the island. Kennedy did not minimize the danger inherent in the standoff. "It shall be the policy of this nation to regard any nuclear missile launched from Cuba against any nation in the Western Hemisphere as an attack by the Soviet Union on the United States, requiring a full retaliatory response upon the Soviet Union."

While the world held its breath, the two sides continued to engage in talks that sources close to the Administration described as tense. Those talks finally bore fruit yesterday in Khrushchev's capitulation.

See "Cuba," p. 5

****

"The Long Run," by Joel Stewart, *Alabama Magazine*, May 2008, pp. 7-8.

As kids in the 1950s, we tore around like crazy. There wasn't much to keep us inside, so we were outside from breakfast to supper with a brief break for lunch, which we knew as dinner.

We lived near a park, and the neighborhood kids met there every morning for baseball games, hide-and-seek adventures, bike races, and every sort of mayhem known to young boys. All of it done at a single speed: lickety-split.

At some point though, the fun (the serendipity, the sheer exuberance) went out of running, and it morphed into something unpleasant, even if beneficial, a necessary evil.

I blame the grownups. First, it was parents and teachers telling us to slow down. "We don't run in the halls," teachers lectured. "Stay in line." "Wait your turn." "No running on the steps." "Slow down." "No running on the sidewalk." "STOP!"

Ironically, our coaches joined in. Instead of encouraging us to run for the joy of it, they touted the benefits (conditioning, stamina) while acknowledging that it was unpleasant. Worse, they used it for punishment. Caught not paying attention: run laps. Late for practice: run laps. How could we not get the message: If running is punishment, it can't be fun.

Perhaps that's why so few kids went out for track. Ours was a small high school anyway, and baseball attracted many of the athletes. But that alone can't explain the scarcity of track athletes. Simply put, running wasn't supposed to be fun and that's all there was to it.

Of course, you had to do some running to get into shape for football and basketball, but that didn't really count. Running was a means to an end. With track, running was means and ends. You ran for conditioning, you ran for practice, and you ran for competition. No, the smart thing was to run away when the subject of track came up.

So, few kids went out for track and nobody, absolutely nobody, came to the meets, not even parents and girlfriends. Where's the glory in that? The football stadium was packed on Friday nights in the fall, and basketball drew good crowds in the winter. Heck, a few parents and girlfriends even showed up for baseball games. Track? The school could have canceled the season, and few would have noticed.

I shouldn't complain. The low interest and thin roster probably explain why the track coach asked me if I'd like to come out in the spring of my junior year. I was available because I had finally accepted that the baseball gods had not been kind to me. The Dodgers would have to look elsewhere for their future first baseman.

I can't speak for anyone else, but I had a blast that spring. I actually learned to enjoy running again. I didn't know what to expect in the beginning. I knew that I wasn't a sprinter. Otherwise, I wouldn't have been playing guard on the football team. As I soon discovered, there were plenty of opportunities available from 440 yards to the mile. (Americans didn't do metric back then.)

Coach Adams tried me at 440 yards, and that's where I stuck. He also penciled me in for a leg on the mile relay team (4 x 440 yards). I also ran the half-mile (880 yards) because we were thin there too.

As it turned out, the mile relay was my favorite event. We were a ragtag bunch: me, a failed baseball player looking for a home; a field athlete who put the shot and threw the discus masquerading as a runner; a sprinter doing penance with the middle-distance misfits; and a baseball player who showed up on meet days to help fill out the roster. But the pairing turned out to be fortuitous. We won every race leading up to the conference championship.

For the conference meet, there were two heats of the mile relay. The results would be based on the combined times from the two heats. Back then, we didn't have fancy timing systems. Just an ordinary sundial. Okay, that was a joke. What we had were coaches with stopwatches.

We ran in the first heat and won handily, still undefeated. But in the second heat, the winning team clocked a faster time. Losing that last race was a disappointment, but life goes on and the disappointments have a way of accumulating. If we're wise, we learn humility and perspective. And with them, how to distinguish between disappointment and loss.

I have enjoyed a good life, but it hasn't been without disappointment and loss. One member of that mile relay team, a good friend, died in Vietnam. I buried my own father a few years ago. Those were losses.

I can still picture that conference championship in my mind after all these years, and I'm still convinced that if we had run in the second heat, we'd have won. But that's not important. It only seemed so at the moment.

Joel Stewart, former City Editor at the *Birmingham Star-Ledger*, is a contributing editor for *Alabama Magazine* and the author of *Crimson Voices: An Oral History of Alabama Football.* He grew up in Grover's Fork, Alabama, surrounded by cotton fields.

CHAPTER 17
THINGS FALL APART

January 15, 1963

Dear Mildred,

Well, the new governor sure threw down the gauntlet yesterday: "Segregation now, segregation tomorrow, and segregation forever." The line, of course, drew a loud response, but I noticed that a lot of those in attendance didn't join in. Earl Thomas wrote our lead article on the inauguration. I added a feature that sampled reactions from around the state.

Our editorial on the inaugural and the new administration was a disgrace. At least in my opinion. Obviously, not everyone agrees. Mac wants to give Wallace the benefit of the doubt. He says that the address was theater. Meant to patronize his supporters. I'm not convinced.

Wallace drew a line in the sand. What's going to happen when someone threatens to breech it? How does he save face? I believe that he's playing with fire and should be called out. Early and often. I just can't figure out how this turns out good. I've done this long enough now that I'd rather not live in such interesting times.

I don't know if you're aware, but Dr. King and the SCLC are planning a campaign for Birmingham for this spring. The governor's statement seems to me to be almost an invitation for violence. Incendiary. That's the word I urged Mac to use to describe the governor's address. Of course, he didn't. I hope that I'm wrong, but I don't think so.

Surely there's some good news. I guess that Alabama beating Oklahoma in the Orange Bowl counts as good news even if it's two weeks old. I'm not exactly a football fan, unless James is playing, but I watched most of the game. Mac was having a watch party, and I surprised myself and went. I've been around long enough that they invite me to these things, but I don't think they really expect me to show up. I fooled them this time, but nobody said boo. I actually enjoyed myself.

I went because, like everyone else, I'm a Joe Namath fan. Coming from western Pennsylvania, you'd think he'd stand out like a sore thumb in Tuscaloosa. But he seems to have won everybody over. Part of that is his athleticism; you have to respect it. He also just exudes what appears to be effortless charm. That's a gift too.

I don't know if this team was as good as the 1961 National Championship team, but it was very good. Without that 7-6 loss to Georgia Tech, they might have been national champs again. I wouldn't be surprised to see them win another championship before Namath graduates in two years.

You'll be happy to hear that I'm getting out more. And it's not just Mac's get-to-gather. I met this reporter from WHOD at a reception earlier this year. Her name is Betty. Betty Howard. She's been at the station since last fall, but our paths hadn't crossed before. She's younger, maybe thirty. I haven't asked. That would be rude. What would really be rude would be if she asked mine.

She's from Illinois. So, a Yankee. She counters that she's from southern Illinois. She graduated from Northwestern, so she's obviously smart. And ambitious. I guess that explains why she came here. The same reason I've stayed all these years. It's ground zero for the most important story of the day. If you're good, it's a chance to get noticed.

I get the impression that she showed up at the reception in order to meet me. She hasn't said that in so many words, but she's hinted at it. See, I'm a legend even if they don't realize it in Grover's Fork yet. I do know that she's been picking my brain ever since. I don't mind though. In fact, I'm flattered. I've watched her on the air, and it's clear that she's going places. I'm happy to help. Especially since it's another woman.

We've met for lunch a couple of times and spent last Saturday comparing notes on Dr. King and the SCLC. She hasn't been here long, but she's done her homework. What she lacks is experience on the front lines. I know that I wasn't prepared for my first riot, but I don't know how you can be. I thought that I knew something about mobs.

Hey, I read *The Crowd in the French Revolution* in college. Shouldn't that have prepared me? Didn't Stephen Crane learn about combat by playing high school football? I covered sorority rush when I was on the society beat. Shouldn't that have prepared me for covering a mob? Of course, I had no clue. I just wanted to curl up in a fetal position my first time.

I'm worried about what will happen in Birmingham with Wallace fanning the flames and Bull Connor "keeping" the peace. Talk about the fox guarding the henhouse. If Betty draws the assignment, I'll worry about her. Being a print reporter, I don't stand out so much. It's hard for television reporters to blend into a crowd. You never know when a mob will decide that the press is part of the enemy. But I can't protect her. Or anybody else. I'll have my hands full just staying safe myself.

I just can't accept that we're still locked in this dance. You and I have discussed this before. The *Brown* decision should have been the last nail in the Jim Crow coffin. Segregation was dead, if not buried yet.

Of course, in retrospect, we should have been wary of the Court's "order" that desegregation should proceed with "all deliberate speed." What does that mean anyway? Obviously, the emphasis has been on the deliberate and not the speed. The delay isn't going to change the outcome. All it's going to do is make the parties even more wary of each other. How can that be a good thing?

As you can tell, I'm getting too old for this beat. The highs and lows aren't good for my health: mental or physical. I wonder if I've gone into adrenaline deficit. Maybe it's time to either move over to the editorial page or maybe back to the society page. If they'll have me.

Sorry for burdening you with my midlife crisis. Yes, midlife! We might as well get used to it. We have crossed the Great Divide of life. Halfway to oblivion. I guess if you believe in Heaven, the Great Divide would be death. But it's much too late in the evening to contemplate that.

Sweet dreams,
Janet

****

"Birmingham Council Yields to Protestors; Pledges End to Jim Crow," by Earl Thomas and Janet Bell, *The Montgomery Observer*, May 10, 1963, p. 1.

The Rev. Fred Shuttlesworth of the Alabama Christian Movement for Human Rights and Dr. Martin Luther King of the Southern Christian Leadership Conference announced yesterday that the City of Birmingham had agreed to desegregate local businesses and public facilities within ninety days, ending a confrontation that began on April 3.

The nearly two-month campaign brought unwanted national and international attention to a city that King called the nation's most segregated. Relying on boycotts and nonviolent marches and sit-ins, the campaign sought to pressure local businesses to end segregation in public facilities and businesses and to open employment to Negroes.

Bull Connor, Birmingham's combative Commissioner of Public Safety, responded to the peaceful marches by turning fire hoses on protestors, including children, using dogs to attack protestors, and ordering mass arrests. Although the tactic of using children in the marches drew criticism from some including Attorney General Robert Kennedy and Negro activist Malcolm X, it succeeded in drawing attention to the campaign.

King was arrested on Good Friday, April 12, and more than 600 school children were arrested on May 2. With the city jails full, Connor turned fire hoses on demonstrators in an attempt to keep them out of downtown.

King defended the protests as "a moral responsibility to disobey unjust laws" in a letter written from jail and defended his involvement in the campaign against critics who labeled him an "outsider."

"Injustice anywhere is a threat to justice everywhere," he noted.

See "Protest," p. 6

****

May 26, 1963

Dear Mildred,

It seems like I've lived a year since January 1, but the calendar still says May. I never expected to be stuck in Birmingham for two months. It was exhausting but something good came out of it. If Birmingham can change, there's hope for us all. I'm not convinced that it's time to celebrate though. The hard work of reconciliation will take time and good faith on both sides, and that's never guaranteed.

I'd like to decompress for a few months, but that's not likely to happen. It looks like the governor is itching for a fight over the integration of the university. Earl and I are already following the story and we'll likely end up in Tuscaloosa in a couple of weeks. Who knows how long we'll be there, but we know how the story ends. I could write the lead today. The only surprise will be in the details.

Mac still contends that Wallace isn't stupid and knows the outcome. He's only interested in saving face with his supporters. He's right that Wallace isn't stupid. So, it follows that he knows, despite all of his rhetoric to the contrary, that he can't win this fight.

Mac's narrative is that Wallace will push the Kennedys to the brink before yielding. That'll make him a hero to his supporters who have always shown an affinity for lost causes. He won't really lose in their eyes. In fact, he'll likely grow in stature. Wallace is exactly the kind of person Dante had in mind when he placed hypocrites near the bottom of hell. The eighth circle, if I'm not mistaken. The final resting place of hypocrites, corrupt politicians, and pimps. He'll be right at home.

While in Birmingham, Earl and I met up with Betty Howard one evening for dinner and a movie. It was weird doing normal things after a day of demonstrations. We went to a place on the south side that seemed like it was a thousand miles away from the chaos downtown. The dinner was relaxing but not the movie. It was a Hitchcock film called *The Birds*. If it ever gets to Grover's Fork, you've got to see it. It's not as terrifying as *Psycho*, but close enough. I still check to see if the door is locked before I take a shower. Now, I'll probably get nervous if I see a flock of birds gathering overhead. That speaks to the genius of Hitchcock.

Betty survived her baptism by fire better than most. She admitted to some fearful moments, but you couldn't tell from her on-camera coverage. Off-camera, she didn't try to hide the stress, and that's a good thing. I've found that it's best to admit it, face it, and move on. The worst thing you can do is to bottle it up and carry it around. It just wears you down.

Okay, this can't all be about me and work. What does James think of The Beach Boys? It seems like every time I turned on the radio in Birmingham, the disc jockey was playing "Surfin' U.S.A." It's certainly catchy, and the vocals sound great. I'm not sure that James and his mates can match The Beach Boys' harmony though. Plus, it would be surreal playing surf music in a gym surrounded by cotton fields.

I'm always jealous of you this time of year. Another week and you'll be off for three months. Three months! It takes me seven years to earn three months of vacation. Right now, I think that I'd trade my Pulitzer and my book royalties for a three-month vacation.

I really want you and James to visit this summer, but I can't tell you when. Everything is going to depend on what happens at the university. So, we'll have to wait and see. I do want you to meet Betty. I think that you'll really like her.

What are James' plans for the summer? In a week, he'll be a rising senior. I honestly can't believe it. It seems so sudden. Has he decided on a college yet? Send him to Huntington. I'll watch out for him.

Hope to see you soon,
Janet

****

"Color Barrier Falls at Capstone; Wallace Yields After Brief Standoff," by Earl Thomas and Janet Bell, *The Montgomery Observer*, June 12, 1963, p. 1.

Alabama Governor George C. Wallace abandoned his attempt to block Negro students from enrolling at the University of Alabama yesterday after a confrontation with the Justice Department. In a bit of political theater, Wallace stood in the door of Foster Auditorium where summer school registration was being held to block Negro students Vivian Malone and James Hood from entering to officially enroll for classes.

Malone and Hood waited in a parked car nearby while the televised drama unfolded. Wallace, who had pledged in his January inaugural address to block the desegregation of Alabama schools, faced off against U.S. Deputy Attorney General Nicolas Katzenbach. Katzenbach reminded Governor Wallace that he was defying a federal district court order to admit Malone and Hood and ordered him to stand aside.

The governor launched into a defiant speech on states' rights. Following a delay, President John F. Kennedy federalized the Alabama National Guard, and Guard Commander General Henry Graham ordered Wallace to stand aside. Wallace finally complied, and Malone and Hood were ushered into Foster Auditorium to register.

The day's drama began early when Malone and Hood arrived at the Birmingham Courthouse to pre-register. They then drove to Foster Auditorium on the university campus in Tuscaloosa where they were to complete their registration and pay their fees.

See "Color Barrier," p. 5

****

June 16, 1963

Dear Janet,

I'm so relieved that things went peacefully in Tuscaloosa. I do worry about you in those situations. I read your reporting. It was much more nuanced than anything else that I read or saw on television.

Why pretend there was any drama in this whole sordid affair? It was clearly staged; that's the story here. It's not news that the university was finally desegregated. Why would anyone think this was going to be any different than Ole Miss last year? No, the news is that the governor staged a sham event. I refuse to call it symbolic. He came, he saw, he folded. He didn't resist. He's not anyone's hero standing firm against the leviathan. At least you and Earl were able to make that point, even if indirectly.

I'm not sure that James and I will be visiting for a while. He'll be spending as much time as he can with Joel. Ernest is closing the picture show on June 30, and Joel's dad will be out of a job. He's looking for a similar job, but that means they'll have to move. Both James and Joel are distraught. They've been best friends since forever. I can't imagine how hard it would have been if you had moved away while we were in high school.

They're keeping the band together for now, but I can tell that their hearts aren't really into the music. Joel suggested that they find another guitarist just in case he has to move, but James won't hear of it. He's in denial. James "digs" The Beach Boys, and the boys just added "Surfin' U.S.A." to their set. And you're right; surf music sounds out of place in rural Alabama.

So does protest music, but James brought home a Bob Dylan album last week. It's called *The Freewheelin' Bob Dylan*. Are you familiar with Dylan? The songs are mostly protest songs. There's even one, "Oxford Town," that's based on James Meredith's enrollment at Ole Miss. You should appreciate that.

My favorite is called "Blowin' in the Wind." If you haven't heard it, you should listen to it. I interpret it to mean that the "truth" (he says "answer") is kinetic and hard to grasp. I like that. Listening to his lyrics, it's hard to believe he's as young as he is.

The boys won't be playing any Dylan though. It's not their style at all. Dylan is acoustic guitar and harmonica. James started out with an acoustic guitar, but he quickly moved on to electric. Rock and roll, right? Anyway, I don't think any of the boys can relate to Dylan's lyrics, much less sing them convincingly. I say that, but they're only a few years younger than he is. Maybe they know more than I imagine; now that's a scary thought.

James is working at Morgan Farms again this summer. Ernest is working overtime to convince him to join the family business after college. James remains noncommittal, so who knows? He doesn't confide that much in me anymore. Why should he? I'm only his mother. (Who's feeling sorry for herself?)

James is going to have some decisions to make soon. He's signed up to take the ACT in September. After that, he'll need to start applying to colleges. Ernest is pushing Auburn. His advice to James is to major in business and minor in agriculture since he'll be running an agriculture-based business if he takes over Morgan Farms. Ernest has even offered to pay for college, but I'm resisting that. Ernest's gifts always come with a price.

Right now, though, with the cloud that's hanging over Joel, James isn't interested in much of anything. I doubt that he'll be excited about a trip to Montgomery. Joel was in Montgomery last week representing Wiregrass County High School at Boys' State. It's usually held at the university, but the American Legion moved it to Huntingdon to avoid the circus created by the governor, so we'll have to wait and see about a visit. Of course, there's no reason you can't come here. I'm sure your parents would love to have you. I know that I would.

Love,
Mildred

****

"Birmingham Church Bombings Leaves Four Dead," by Philip Hardin, *The Wiregrass Herald*, September 16, 1963, p. 1.

(SPA) Birmingham, Alabama. Four young Negro girls died Sunday morning when a bomb exploded at Birmingham's 16th Street Baptist Church. Another twenty-two people were injured in the powerful blast that left a crater five feet wide and two feet deep.

The victims, Addie Mae Collins (14), Carol Denise McNair (11), Carole Robertson (14), and Cynthia Wesley (14), were changing into their choir gowns in the church basement at the time of the blast. The bomb, constructed of dynamite, went off at appropriately 10:22 a.m. when the church was full for Sunday service.

Thousands of Negroes gathered at the church in the aftermath of the bombing, and the church's pastor, Rev. John Cross, Jr., tried to defuse the situation by reciting the 23rd Psalm. Nevertheless, scattered violence erupted into the evening. The Birmingham City Council met in emergency session but refrained from ordering a curfew. Governor George Wallace ordered 300 state troopers to the city to help quell the unrest.

Coming so soon after the Birmingham Campaign succeeded in securing a pledge from the city to desegregate, the bombing is another black eye for the city. Mayor Albert Boutwell described the bombing as "just sickening," and pledged a thorough investigation.

U.S. Attorney General Robert Kennedy also ordered twenty-five FBI agents to Birmingham to assist in the investigation.

See "Church Bombing," p. 3

****

September 18, 1963

Dear Janet,

Will this madness never end? Four little girls in church. Who bombs a church? I blame Wallace for fanning the flames, but he's not alone. Where have our "leaders" been the past few years? Not leading, that's for sure. I don't mean just the politicians, but business leaders, school leaders, church leaders: They all bear some responsibility. People deserve better. All people regardless of color.

The State is being condemned far and wide, and we deserve it. I hate it. I'm embarrassed by it. But it's the bed we've made. I'm not equating everyone with whoever planted the bomb. I hope only a few are that evil.

Too many have contributed by voting for intolerance. Others by remaining silent. I admit to being one of the latter. I've convinced myself that if I do no harm, then I'm still on the side of the angels. I'm trying to be more honest with myself. The one thing I can be proud of is that I've taught James to be tolerant. (I think I have anyway.)

James has stopped moping so much about Joel's move to Atlanta. I hoped that once school started, he'd begin to snap out of it, and he has. The football team looks like it's going to be really good, and that helps. He's moved from end to halfback on offense and likes running with the ball. He also moved to linebacker on defense. So far, they've won both their games by lopsided scores.

Instead of dissolving the band after Joel moved, he finally agreed to keep it going. They recruited a guitarist to replace Joel, and I think they sound as good as before. They already have a commitment to play the homecoming dance next month.

The other big news is that the ACT test is coming up in a couple of weeks. I've even managed to get James to do some test prep; not a lot, but any is better than none. If I had to guess, I'd say his first choice of college is Auburn. He's still considering Alabama since that's Joel's first (and only) choice. He's even mentioned Troy State, but that's not happening.

He and Joel have kept in touch since Joel moved in July, but the letters are getting more sporadic. Maybe that's because James is in love. He's had girlfriends before, but not like this. I doubt that you know her. Her name is Marie Walker, and they moved here after the war. She's been a perfect antidote for Joel's absence. They're in that early bright-hot stage now, so we'll see how it goes. She's smart, cute, and sweet, so Mom's not complaining.

How's Betty? Is she still keeping you busy? I catch her occasionally on the WHOD newscast. She is very good. I can't imagine that she'll stay in Montgomery for long.

Come for Homecoming if you can.

Love,
Mildred

****

November 10, 1963

Dear Joel,

Hey, it's me. Sorry I haven't written lately, but you know how it is. Now that football is over, I'll have more time. Believe it or not but we beat everybody but Barbour County. We should have beaten them too. The game was over there, and Clay didn't play because of the flu. It's hard to win on the road against a tough team without your starting quarterback. It would have been nice to finish undefeated our senior year though.

To tell the truth, I don't think I'll miss football that much. I'm not saying that I didn't have fun playing. I'm saying that I'm ready to move on. Plus, next August when the guys are sweating through two-a-days, I'll be sitting in the shade with a glass of iced tea.

How'd you guys finish up? I'm sure that the competition in Atlanta is tougher than what we face here in the Wiregrass.

We got our ACT scores back last week. I made 29. Better than I expected. It was the second-highest score in the class, but of course, we expected that. Cheryl Wells made 30. Of course, we expected that. You were the only one of us who might have beaten her. How did you do? If it's 31 or above, I'll let Cheryl know for sure. Since we got our scores back, she's been strutting around even more than usual.

Are you still planning to go to Alabama? I'm going to apply to Auburn for sure. Mom wants me to apply to Birmingham-Southern. She and Aunt Janet went there and think it's the best school in the state. Grandpa is pushing Auburn. He wants me to come back here after college and work with him until he retires, and then, I'd take over. It's tempting. I'd never have to worry about money. I know from working on the farm all these years that it's something I can do.

The truth is I'm really not interested in anything else other than music, but I'm not crazy. I know that's not happening. Mom doesn't want me to work with Grandpa. She's never liked him, but he's been okay to me. At least I don't have to decide anytime soon, so we'll see.

The band is still together. We got Jerry Mercer to replace you. He's actually pretty good. We played the homecoming dance again this year. They gave us $100. See what you're missing.

Are you still dating that cheerleader you told me about? What was her name? Marie and I are still together, but I'm not convinced her heart is in it. Or mine for that matter. I don't know what happened. She seemed so perfect last summer.

Anyway, she's planning to go to Troy State next year. So, we're going in different directions. Maybe we're just marking time until then. I'd like to get beyond second base just once before we break up though.

Classes are boring as usual. Surprisingly, physics isn't bad. I'm taking typing with the secretarial students because I thought it might help in college, so that's interesting. There are only a few of us guys and all those girls. It's the smartest thing I've done in school. I hate trig, and English with Mrs. Burch is a joke. You know more English than she does.

Being a senior isn't as much fun as I expected. I'm ready to be done and to move on, but that's still months off.

Write when you get a chance, let me know your ACT score.

Yours,
James

****

"President Assassinated in Dallas; Suspect in Custody" by Neil Harris, *The Wiregrass Herald,* November 23, 1963, p. 1.

(SPA) Dallas, Texas. President John F. Kennedy was pronounced dead at 12:30 p.m. yesterday at Parkland Memorial Hospital in Dallas. The President was shot while riding in a motorcade through Dealey Plaza in downtown Dallas.

Texas Governor John Connally who was riding in Kennedy's limousine was also wounded in the attack. First Lady Jacqueline Kennedy and Connally's wife, Nellie, were passengers in the limousine but were unharmed.

Dallas police captured Kennedy's alleged assassin, Lee Harvey Oswald, shortly after the shooting. Oswald has been charged with the murders of Kennedy and Dallas policeman, J.D. Tippit, and is being held at the city jail on the fourth floor of Dallas Police Headquarters. Police say that Oswald maintains his innocence and insists that he has been set up. Investigators warn that it's too early to speculate about motive.

Kennedy's body was returned to Washington, D.C., on Air Force One a few hours after the assassination. Vice President Lyndon B. Johnson accompanied the body and was sworn in as the 36th President of the United States while aboard the presidential jet.

See "Assassination," p. 3

See "Assassination," p. 3

****

December 31, 1963

Dear Janet,

Well, it's another New Year's Eve at home alone for me. James is out with Marie. I'm not crazy about him being out tonight, but he'll be 18 years old at midnight. I can't hold on forever. He promised to be careful, but what's he going to say? I probably won't relax until I hear the car pull into the driveway.

I'm feeling melancholic this evening. Maybe it's being alone on New Year's Eve, which is my own fault. This is who I've become, for better or worse. After next summer, James will be off to college, and I'll be stuck here by myself. I shouldn't complain to you since you've managed on your own since college. But I'm not as independent as you've always been. I guess that I'll have to learn.

I've also been thinking about Roger today. He will have been missing for ten years on Thursday. I've talked with Ernest's lawyer, and we're going to petition to have Roger declared legally deceased.

I don't know if anything will actually change. Well, James will become Ernest and Glenda's most direct heir. I guess that means that he'll be rich one day, but who knows? I'd rather that James earns his way in the world, but that's out of my hands.

I just wish that we knew what happened to Roger; all these years and nothing. I'm still convinced that he's alive somewhere. Of course, there's never been anything to suggest that's the case. On the other hand, there's never been anything to suggest otherwise.

Wherever he is, I hope he's found some peace. Yes, he abandoned James and me, but I really don't think he believed that he had a choice. Anyway, ours wasn't exactly a happy marriage so much as a convenient marriage. Even so, it would be easier to let it go if I had some closure, real closure, not just legal closure, but after all this time, I've given up on that happening.

New Year's Eve is a time to look forward, but I'm having a hard time imagining anything good following 1963. It's not just the assassination of President Kennedy, or the spectacle of Governor Wallace blocking the schoolhouse door, or Bull Connor's police dogs, or the coup in South Vietnam. We are now even deeper in that mess, and James has to register for the draft next month.

I know that good things happened in 1963 too. But sitting here alone on New Year's Eve, all I seem to recall are the bad, and I'm not even drinking. Maybe I should be.

I'm sure that everything will look better tomorrow in the light of a new year, a fresh start. That's a myth too, isn't it? We can never really start over, just like we can never go back. (The arrow of time and all that.) I've always been amazed at how insignificant we really are. We drop in at some random moment in time, have our little hour, and are done forever.

You couldn't help but have noticed the Millay allusion in the last sentence? I don't read her enough. I go back to Miss Emily quite a lot, but I seldom revisit Millay. She's not as droll as Dickinson, but she can be quite interesting in her own way. One might think the two are exact opposites, but I sometimes wonder if they didn't share more than meets the eye. On the other hand, I don't see Miss Emily burning her candle at both ends. Despite "Wild Nights!" I guess that's why I identify more with Miss Emily; my candle isn't putting off much heat, or light for that matter.

Enough of me feeling sorry for myself. What of you? I hope that, unlike me, you're out celebrating New Year's; people are the best antidote for melancholia.

Here's to a Happy 1964 despite my misgivings.

Love,
Mildred

P.S. Have you heard the single from the British group called The Beatles? I'm listening to WLS, and the deejay just played it. It's called "I Want to Hold Your Hand." James heard the song on the day after Christmas, and he drove over to Centerville on Saturday to buy a copy; just like that, nobody else matters to him, not Elvis, not The Beach Boys, not anybody. We'll see if they last. I do like the two songs of theirs that I've heard, but I wonder if Americans really want rock and roll with a British accent.

CHAPTER 18
A PLACE TO REST

February 12, 1964

Dear Mildred,

Yes, I was watching *Ed Sullivan* on Sunday night. Who wasn't? I think we now have the answer to your question about rock and roll with a British accent. I saw in the paper that 73,000,000 viewers watched *Sullivan* Sunday night. I doubt most of them were there for Ed. I think The Beatles will be around for a while. Watch out, the next thing you know James will be growing his hair longer. Ha.

Is James any closer to deciding about college? I think he'll be fine wherever he goes. You and I were more comfortable in a smaller setting than Auburn or Alabama, but James seems more extroverted than we were at that age. Or any age to be honest. So he should fit in anywhere. Auburn might be his best choice. Decent academics, an active social scene, and close to Mom!

Work has been a bit of a grind lately. The governor is so predictable that he's hardly news anymore. Most everybody's attention right now is elsewhere: the presidential contest, the civil rights bill before Congress, and the unfolding drama in Vietnam. The election looks to be Johnson's to lose. Especially if the Republicans nominate Goldwater. The pure choice is seldom the best choice if the goal is to win. Despite the certain filibuster, the goal line is in sight for the civil rights bill. After that, even Wallace will have to acknowledge defeat. Right?

That leaves the situation in Vietnam. I had lunch with Col. Deal from the Air War College last week, and he thinks we're being drawn even deeper into the conflict. I should say Prof. Deal since he's been retired for a while now. Even so, he can only say so much, even off the record, but it's clear to me that there's more going on there than we're being told. At least if things escalate, James will have a draft deferment while in college. Whatever happens, this should blow over before he graduates. So, try not to worry too much, Mom.

When does the Court rule on your petition to have Roger declared legally dead? I know that won't necessarily give you closure, but it's something. I keep thinking that he'll turn up one day with a story about amnesia or something. But ten years is a long time. Maybe we'll never know. I wish he'd left a note.

What are your plans for Valentine's? Wasn't it last year that you spent the evening reading Emily Dickenson? You said that James' band is playing at a Valentine's dance at the high school. Maybe you should volunteer to chaperone. Whatever you do, don't drink the punch.

I'll likely stay home and watch television. Betty is anchoring the 10:00 p.m. news, and everybody else I know seems to be part of a twosome. I promise I won't be reading Miss Emily on Valentine's. I still haven't read one of the books you gave me for Christmas. I finished *The Group* before New Year's. I can't say that I loved it. It was pretty dark. But I did identify with it, and I'm glad I read it.

That leaves the Muriel Spark novel, *The Girls of Slender Means*. Why do you always give me these novels about young women making their way in the big city? Maybe one day I'll write my own. Montgomery, of course, is not New York or London. I bet the stories are the same though.

Anyway, let's make plans for you to visit over spring break. You don't need to bring James. He won't burn the house down if you leave him alone.

Love,
Janet

****

May 9, 1964

Dear Janet,

James is off to prom with Marie. I guess the countdown to graduation has officially begun. He did look handsome. He and Marie have been dating much this past year. I'm happy that they're still together for prom. They seemed to run out of gas before Christmas, but they've stayed together. I doubt that their relationship will survive beyond this summer, but they'll have this memory.

I'm trying to be happy for James without being sad for myself. I am proud of him too, but tonight is just another reminder that he'll be gone soon. I've never lived alone. I'm not sure that I know how. Even after college, I lived at home until my wedding day, so my whole life, there have been people around.

Now that Roger is legally dead, you could say that I'm available again, but at forty-two, I'm too set in my ways to live with another man. I was more malleable when I married Roger. Not to mention naïve and perhaps a bit desperate. It's one thing to be single in Montgomery and quite another in Grover's Fork, as you well know. Mom was never less than subtle about it, but I knew her expectations. I did like Roger; he was attractive, respectable, and available. Plus, he was kind and thoughtful. That was refreshing. He also was vulnerable, but I missed that at the start.

I thought that Roger would be my port in the storm. I felt fragile, and I imagined that he would shelter me from the slings and arrows of outrageous fortune, or at least small-town gossip. Too late, I realized that he was more fragile than I am. I can't complain. He gave me James, and James has been my shield ever since. I guess that's why I'm so ambivalent about him leaving. I know that he'll be fine. It's me I'm not so sure of, and I thought that Roger needed help.

James is planning to work for Ernest again this summer. Ernest has been a mellower misanthrope lately. I think part of it is that James is going to Auburn. Ernest thinks that's a sign that he's won the battle of bringing him back here to take over the farm operation. We'll see. I hope not, but it's James' decision.

I'm afraid that Ernest is going to try to bribe James with a new car for graduation. He bought James a Beetle when he turned sixteen against my wishes. Well, James has fallen for that new Ford, the Mustang. Have you seen one? They've just started selling them in Centerville. There's already one here in town. One of the young teachers at the school bought one. I must say that it's sporty.

James has a perfectly good car. The best thing about it is that it doesn't go very fast. The Mustang looks like it goes very fast. I love him, but he's still a teenager. Anyway, he mentioned the Mustang to Ernest at Sunday dinner, and Ernest asked a lot of questions. He didn't make any commitment, but I know Ernest. I caught his eye and shook my head, but he didn't respond. How can I tell James he can't accept a graduation present from his grandfather?

At least Ernest seems to have accepted that we won't need his help with college expenses. I've been saving for this since Roger disappeared, and James has put away some money from his earnings over the years to help, so we should be fine.

Graduation is Friday night, May 29, at 7:00. Graduation gift is optional. Your presence is not.

See you soon,
Mildred

****

"President Signs Civil Rights Act of 1964," by John Moody, *The Wiregrass Herald*, July 3, 1964, p. 1.

(SPA) Washington, D.C. President Lyndon B. Johnson signed the landmark Civil Rights Act of 1964 yesterday in the White House East Room before a Who's Who of legislators, government officials, and civil rights leaders including Dr. Martin Luther King, Jr., Senator Robert F. Kennedy, and FBI Director J. Edgar Hoover.

The legislation, which was first introduced by the Kennedy Administration in 1963, outlaws discrimination based on race, color, religion, sex, or national origin in education, employment, and public accommodations.

Following Kennedy's assassination, President Johnson revived the stalled legislation and lobbied Congress to pass the measure. The House of Representatives passed the bill overwhelmingly in February, but Southern Democrats in the Senate launched a 54-day filibuster.

The Senate finally voted cloture on June 19, and the legislation was approved by a lopsided 72-27 margin. The cloture vote was the first time in history that the Senate defeated a filibuster of a civil rights bill.

In remarks after the signing, President Johnson recalled the patriots who signed the *Declaration of Independence* and noted that America's "unending search for justice" continues with the passage of this legislation. The President pointed out that "the great majority of American citizens" support the Civil Rights Act and pledged that his administration would enforce the law "without delay."

See "Civil Rights," p. 3

****

July 5, 1964

Dear Mildred,

Happy Fourth! I'm a day late, but don't complain. I spent much of yesterday at the paper working on an opinion piece on the Civil Rights Act. How we got here, where we go now. It's in this morning's paper. I'm happy with it. The term "landmark" is probably overused, but I think it applies in this case.

This is the culmination of years of struggle and should squeeze the last life out of Jim Crow. Unlike *Brown*, this is comprehensive, and LBJ seems determined to enforce it. Notice that the Act doesn't offer hope to those who would defer action. There's no "with all deliberate speed" here. Let's just hope we get this right. They say that the devil is in the details, so we'll see. But I'm optimistic.

Afterward, I dropped by Mac's house for a Fourth cookout. Betty is finally off the weekend shift, and she tagged along. I guess there were about fourteen of us. There was lots of beer and more than enough fireworks.

Boys will be boys. Even when they have grandchildren. I've never understood the fascination with noise. And that's all there is with these backyard variety fireworks. There's no light show or anything remotely interesting. Oh, well. I kept my mouth shut. Anyway, the food was good, the beer was cold, and the evening was pleasant.

What did you and James do for the Fourth? I'm guessing that James was out since it was not only the Fourth but also a Saturday night. Has the new Mustang had an effect on his social life? How about speeding tickets? Ha. It is a striking car. If I were ten years younger, I'd consider getting one myself. Okay, fifteen years younger.

I've been thinking about writing a piece linking the Mustang to the postwar generation. There are a lot of them, and they are having an outsize impact on popular culture. Up until now, the popularity of rock and roll music has been the most obvious manifestation, but I think there's more coming. Lots more.

When is James scheduled for Freshman Orientation at Auburn? I would imagine any time now. I bet he's getting excited. College is a big step even if you're not going that far away. In reality, 100 miles might as well be 1000 for all the control parents have. Do freshmen at Auburn get to have cars? Live off-campus? Of course, the girls can't. They have to be locked in dorms or sorority houses with strict curfews. To protect them, of course. Funny, I never felt protected. Mostly confined. Maybe that's one of the things this generation will change.

While James is at Freshman Orientation, why don't you visit for a few days? Get you out of the house and out of Grover's Fork. It'll do you good. No maybes, I want a promise.

Enjoy the heat and humidity.

Love,
Janet

****

"Congress Passes War Resolution," by John Moody, *The Wiregrass Herald*, August 8, 1964, p. 1.

(SPA) Washington, D.C. Congress yesterday passed overwhelmingly the Gulf of Tonkin Resolution giving President Lyndon B. Johnson broad powers to respond to North Vietnamese attacks against U.S. forces.

The Administration asked for the joint resolution following two recent attacks on U.S. Naval vessels by North Vietnamese torpedo boats in the waters of the Gulf of Tonkin off the coast of North Vietnam. The initial attack came on August 2 and targeted the USS Maddox, a destroyer. The Maddox and a second destroyer, the USS Turner Joy were attacked on August 4.

Following the second attack, President Johnson ordered air attacks against the bases from which the torpedo boats were launched. Addressing the attacks on August 4, the President justified the response: "Repeated acts of violence against the armed forces of the United States must be met not only with alert defense but with positive reply." He also asked Congress to approve a war resolution giving him authority "for all necessary action to protect our Armed Forces." At the same time, he repeated assurances that "the United States seeks no wider war."

The House of Representatives approved the resolution unanimously, while the Senate voted 98-2 in favor with Senators Wayne Morse (D-OR) and Ernest Gruening (D-AK) in opposition. In defending his "NO" vote, Senator Gruening warned against "sending our American boys into combat in a war in which we have no business, which is not our war, into which we have been misguidedly drawn, which is steadily being escalated."

See "War Resolution," p. 4

****

August 10, 1964

Dear Janet,

I'm sure that you saw the story about the Gulf of Tonkin Resolution. What does it mean? It looks to me like Congress gave LBJ a blank check to start a war in Vietnam. How is that right? We're trusting one man with the power to go to war? I'm sure that's not what the Founding Fathers had in mind.

I've spoken to a couple of people here, but nobody seems too concerned. They're not even sure exactly where or what Vietnam is. They just don't take it seriously. Why should they? Nobody has told them much about it.

I've been reading about the French war to restore colonial control over Vietnam after the defeat of Japan. After almost a decade of fighting, the French withdrew. That tells me that a war in Vietnam wouldn't be the cakewalk everyone seems to expect.

I chanced upon a novel by Graham Greene called *The Quiet American* set during the French War. Have you heard of it? It was published in the mid-1950s, but it's no less relevant today, maybe more so. The narrator is a British war correspondent, and the quiet American is a CIA agent already operating in the background there. The whole point is that we don't know what we're doing in places like Indochina. I don't want James sacrificed for other people's arrogance and ambition.

I lost Roger. I can't lose James. Yes, I have my parents, but who knows for how much longer? James is my port in a storm; he always has been. Even when Roger disappeared, it was James' presence that kept me going.

I know that I worry too much. James is going to Auburn next month, not to the Army. I spend too much time alone, that's all. James works all day and goes out most evenings. I can't say anything though. I don't want to be clingy. I know he wants to see his friends as much as possible before he leaves for school.

I'm actually surprised that anyone tolerates me, even you, my oldest and closest friend. I bet Betty isn't as high maintenance as I am. To be honest, I'm a bit jealous that you've found such a dear friend, but I can't complain. I've never tried very hard. So, if I'm lonely, it's my own damned fault. Anyway, it's hard not to like Betty. I have to say that you're lucky in your friends. Ha-ha!

They're playing "The Little Old Lady From Pasadena" on the radio. Maybe I should borrow James' Mustang and go speeding through Grover's Fork. Not exactly what anyone would expect of the local librarian. The truth is, I've never stepped out of character. Never. Even when we went away to college, I stuck to the script. I always admired you for being able to change the script when it suited you. I guess that I never had the confidence to do that. That's why I'll never have a billboard out on the edge of town.

Oh, I hear James' Mustang now. He's home early tonight. It must have been a tough day on the farm. Or maybe he just misses his mom.

Love,
Mildred

****

"Dems Nominate LBJ; Humphrey Will Be Running Mate," by Jake Hollings, *The Wiregrass Herald,* August 27, 1964, p. 1.

(SPA) Atlantic City, N.J. The Democratic National Convention last night nominated President Lyndon B. Johnson as its standard-bearer for the November election. There was little drama in last night's vote, which felt more like a coronation for the President.

Little drama is expected tonight as the convention fills out the ticket with a vice-presidential nominee. Sources close to the President indicate that his choice for running mate is Senator Hubert

H. Humphrey of Minnesota, and all indications are that the Convention will affirm the President's choice.

A Johnson-Humphrey ticket will square off in the fall campaign against the Republican pairing of Arizona Senator Barry Goldwater and New York Representative William E. Miller. Goldwater won the Republican nomination in a bruising battle with New York Governor Nelson A. Rockefeller.

In his acceptance speech, Johnson touted the passage of the Civil Rights Act of 1964, which Senator Goldwater opposed, and outlined a reform agenda that he dubbed "The Great Society." He also painted his opponent as an extremist, repeating Gov. Rockefeller's criticism of Goldwater's "extremism" during the primaries.

With a divided party following a divisive convention, Senator Goldwater faces an uphill battle against a popular incumbent.

See "LBJ," p. 6

****

The Wiregrass Herald   August 31, 1964 p. 12

OBITUARIES

James Chester Morgan, age 18, of Grover's Fork, was killed on Saturday, August 29, when his car struck a freight train in rural Wiregrass County. The accident remains under investigation according to Wiregrass County Sheriff Wayne Smith. James was born January 1, 1946, in Centerville, Alabama. He is survived by his mother, Mildred Morgan, of Grover's Fork; paternal grandparents, Ernest and Glenda Morgan, of rural Wiregrass County; maternal grandparents, Rhone and Marsha Rice, of Grover's Fork; two aunts;

and several cousins. He was preceded in death by his father, Roger Morgan, and uncle, Joseph Morgan.

A 1964 graduate of Grover's Fork High School, James was a member of the football and track teams and was president of the Beta Club, a scholastic honorary. James was the founder, lead guitarist, and vocalist of the popular local rock band, The North Street Boys. He planned to enroll at Auburn University in September.

Visitation is from 4:00 p.m. until 7:00 p.m. today at Walker's Funeral Home in Centerville. A funeral service will be held at 11:00 a.m. tomorrow at the Grover's Fork First Methodist Church with burial following at Grover's Fork Municipal Cemetery.

ABOUT THE AUTHOR

 Tom Miller was born and raised in the Alabama Wiregrass when cotton was still king and mostly picked by hand. He attended the University of Alabama, did a stint in the U.S. Army, and eventually settled in corn country, a.k.a. Iowa, where he taught history at Scott Community College in Bettendorf. He is the author of six novels for middle-grade readers and scores of articles, essays, and reviews for journals, magazines, and newspapers. He also served for fifteen years on the Board of Directors of the Children's Literature Festival. Now retired, Tom lives in Bettendorf with his wife of forty-one years, Connie. They have a son, David, and two grandsons, Dylan and Ryan.